"These stories just keep getting better and better. . . . Every single one of them leaves you wanting more!"

—*Ramblings From This Chick*

BEING ME
Book Two

"A crazy, emotional roller-coaster ride. . . . I was glued to the pages."

—*Fiction Vixen*

"Brilliantly beautiful in its complexity. . . . This book had my heart racing."

—*Scandalicious Book Reviews*

"Breathtaking in its suspense and intrigue."

—HeroesandHeartbreakers.com

IF I WERE YOU
Book One

"This book's plot will keep readers guessing."

—*RT Book Reviews*

"Leaves you begging for more!"

—*Tough Critic Book Reviews*

"This book is incredible. I loved it. *If I Were You* made my pulse pound, my insides clench, and left me breathless. Lisa Renee Jones writes a dark and edgy erotica that hit all my buttons just right."

—*Romantic Book Affairs*

"Absolutely enthralling. . . . Jones has me eating in the palm of her hand."

—*Under the Covers Book Blog*

Escaping Reality

LISA RENEE JONES

G

Gallery Books

New York   London   Toronto   Sydney   New Delhi

G

Gallery Books
An Imprint of Simon & Schuster, Inc.
1230 Avenue of the Americas
New York, NY 10020

First Gallery Books trade paperback edition May 2015

GALLERY BOOKS and colophon are registered trademarks
of Simon & Schuster, Inc.

For information about special discounts for bulk purchases,
please contact Simon & Schuster Special Sales at 1-866-506-1949
or business@simonandschuster.com.

The Simon & Schuster Speakers Bureau can bring authors to your
live event. For more information or to book an event, contact
the Simon & Schuster Speakers Bureau at 1-866-248-3049
or visit our website at www.simonspeakers.com.

Design by Davina Mock Maniscalco

Manufactured in the United States of America

10   9   8   7   6   5   4   3   2   1

Library of Congress Cataloging-in-Publication Data

Jones, Lisa Renee.
Escaping reality / Lisa Renee Jones.—First Gallery Books trade paperback
edition.
    pages cm. (The secret life of Amy Bensen)
  I. Title.
PS3610.O627E 83   2015
813'.6—dc23
                                        2014043482

ISBN 978-1-4767-9382-5
ISBN 978-1-4767-9377-1 (ebook)

*To Diego and Julie for sharing many wonderful weekends
in Denver, and specifically the Cherry Creek area,
to help bring the world in this series come to life.*

ACKNOWLEDGMENT

To Diego for helping me plot this story when sometimes all the twists and turns had me twisting and turning!

ONE

Amy

MY NAME IS ALL THAT'S WRITTEN on the plain white envelope taped to the mirror. It wasn't there when I entered the ladies' room at Manhattan's Metropolitan Museum of Art.

The laughter and pleasure of tonight's charity event evaporate as fear and dread slam into me, adrenaline shooting through my body. No. No. *No.* This can't be happening—but it is.

Suddenly the room begins to fade, and everything goes gray. It's been years since I had a flashback, and I try to fight it, but I'm already right there in it. The scent of smoke burns my nose. The sound of blistering screams shreds my nerves. And all the pain and heartache, the loss of all I once had and will never have again, threatens to overwhelm me.

Fighting the meltdown, I swallow hard and shove away the gut-wrenching memories. I can't let this happen. Not here, in a public place. Not when I'm certain that danger is knocking on my door.

On wobbly knees, clumsy in the four-inch black strappy heels that made me feel sexy only minutes ago, I step forward and press my palms to the counter. I can't seem to make myself reach for the envelope, and my gaze goes to my image in the mirror—to the long, white-blond hair I've worn down tonight in honor of the heritage of my Swedish mother that I'm tired of denying. Gone, too, are the dark-rimmed glasses I've often used to hide the pale blue eyes my parents shared, making it too easy for me to see the empty shell of a person I've become. If this is what I am at twenty-four years old, what will I be like at thirty-four?

Voices sound outside the door, and I yank the envelope from the mirror and rush into a stall. Two women enter the bathroom, and I tune out their gossip about some man they've been admiring at the party. Leaning against the wall, I open the sealed envelope to remove a plain white note-card, and a small key drops to the floor. Cursing my shaking hands, I bend down and scoop it up. For a moment, I can't seem to stand up. I force myself to my feet and blink away the burning sensation in my eyes to read the few short sentences typed on the card.

```
I've found you, and so can they. Go
directly to JFK airport. Do not go home.
Do not linger. Locker 111 will have
everything you need.
```

My heart thunders in my chest as I take in the signature: a triangle with some writing inside. The same symbol that was tattood on the arm of the stranger who saved my life and helped me start a new one—and who'd made sure I understood that seeing that symbol means that I'm in danger and I have to run.

I squeeze my eyes shut, fighting a wave of emotion. Once again, my life is about to be turned upside down. Once again, I will lose everything—and while it's so much less than before, it's all I have. I crumple the note in my hand, desperate to make this all go away. After six years of hiding, I'd dared to believe I was safe—but that was a mistake. Deep down I've known that, ever since I left my job two months ago as a research assistant at the central library to work at the museum. Being here is treading water too close to the bridge.

Straightening, I listen as the women leave and the room goes silent. Anger erupts inside me at the idea that my life is about to be stolen from me again. Inhaling, I tear the note into tiny pieces, flush them down the toilet, and shove the envelope into the trash. I want to throw away the key, too, but some part of me won't let that happen.

Unzipping my small black purse, I drop the key inside. I'm going to finish my party. And maybe I'm going to finish my life right here in New York City. The note didn't say I'd been found; it only warned me that I *could* be found. I don't want to run again. I need time to think, to process, and that is going to have to wait until after the party.

Decision made, I exit the stall, cutting my eyes away from the mirror. I don't want to see myself right now, when I have no idea who "I" am or will be tomorrow. In the numb zone I've used as a survival tool before, almost as many times as I've tried to find the meaning of that symbol on the note, I follow the soft hum of orchestral music, entering a room with a high, oval ceiling decorated with magnificent murals. I tell myself to get lost in the crush of patrons in business attire and waiters offering champagne and finger foods, but I don't. I simply stand there, mourning the new life I've just begun, and that I know is now gone. My "zone" has failed me.

"Amy, where have you been?"

Chloe Monroe, the only person I've let myself consider a friend in years, steps in front of me, a frown on her heart shaped face. From the dark brown curls bouncing around her shoulders to her outgoing personality and fun, flirty attitude, she is my polar opposite, and I love that about her. Now I will lose her. Now I will lose *me*, again.

"Well," she prods when I don't reply quickly enough, shoving her hands onto her hips, "where have you been?"

"The ladies' room. There was a line." I hate how easily the lie comes to me, how it defines me. A lie is all I am.

Chloe's brow furrows. "Hmmm. There wasn't one when I was there. I guess I got lucky." She waves off the thought. "Sabrina's freaking out over some donation paperwork she can't find and says she needs you. I thought you were doing research—when did you start handling donor paperwork?"

"Last week, when she got overwhelmed," I say, and perk up at the idea that my new boss needs me. I need to be needed, even if it's just for tonight. "Where is she?"

"By the front desk." She laces her arm through mine and pulls me forward. "And I'm tagging along with you. I have a sixty-year-old admirer who's bordering on stalker. I need to escape before he hunts me down."

Her light words go deep. *I'm* the one being hunted. I'd thought I was safe—but I'm not, and neither is anyone around me. I've lived that firsthand. I felt that heartache and loss and while being alone sucks, losing someone you care about is far worse.

I stop dead in my tracks and pull Chloe around to face me. "Tell Sabrina I'm getting the forms and will be right there."

"Oh. Okay. Sure." Chloe lets go of my arm, and for a moment I fight the urge to hug her. That would make her seem important to me, and someone could be watching. I turn away and rush for a doorway, feeling sick to my stomach that I'll never see her again.

I finally exit at the side of the building into the muggy August evening and head for a line of cabs, consciously not rushing or looking around me. I've learned ways to avoid attention. Going to work for a place with a direct link to the world I'd left behind wasn't one of them, and now I'm paying for that luxury.

"JFK airport," I say as I slide into the back of a cab and rub the back of my neck at a familiar prickling sensation. A feeling I'd felt often my first year on my own, when I'd been certain danger waited for me around every corner. Hunted. I'm being hunted. All the denial I own won't change my reality.

THE RIDE TO the airport is thirty minutes, and it takes me another fifteen to figure out what the location of locker 111 is once I'm inside the terminal. I pull it open and see a carry-on roller suitcase and a smaller brown leather tote bag with a large yellow envelope sticking up from inside it. Having no desire to be watched while I explore what's been left for me, I gather up the bags and head for a ladies' room.

Once again in a stall, I pull down the baby-changing table and check the contents of the envelope on top. There is a file folder, a bank card, a cell phone, a passport, a note-card, and another small, sealed envelope. I reach for the note first.

There is cash in the bank account, and
the PIN is 1850. I'll add more as you need
it until you get fully settled. You'll
find a new Social Security card, driver's
license, and passport as well. You have a
complete history to memorize, and a résumé
and job history that will check out if
looked into. Throw out your cell phone.
The new one is registered under your new
name and address. There's a plane ticket

```
and the keys to an apartment. Toss all
identification and don't use your bank
account or credit cards. Be smart. Don't
link yourself to your past. Stay away from
museums this time.
```

A new name. That's what stands out to me. *I'm getting another new name. No. No. No.* My heart races at the idea. I don't want another new name. Once again, I'm losing part of myself. After living a lie for years, I'm losing the only part of my fake identity I'd really accepted as me.

I grab the passport and flip it open, and my hand trembles at the sight of the current photo. How did this stranger I met only one time get a picture this recent? I'd once considered him my guardian angel, but I'm freaked out by this. Has he been watching me all this time? I shiver at the idea.

My only comfort is that my first name won't change. I'm now Amy Bensen, rather than Amy Reynolds. I'm still Amy. It's the one piece of good news in all of this and I cling to it, using it to stave off the meltdown I feel coming. I just have to hold it together until I get on the plane. Then I can sink into my seat and think myself into my numb zone, which I can't seem to find right now.

Flipping open the folder, I find an airline ticket. I'm going to Denver, and I leave in an hour. I've never been anywhere but Texas and New York. All I know about Denver is it's big, it's cold, and it's the next place I will pretend is home, when in reality I have no home. The thought makes my chest pinch, but the fear of what might await me if I don't run pushes me past it.

I turn off my cell phone so it won't ping and stuff it, with everything but my new ID and plane ticket, back into the envelope. I have my own money in the bank, and I'm not about to get rid of my identification and access to that resource. Besides, the idea of using a bank card that allows me to be tracked bothers me. I'll be visiting the bank tomorrow and removing any cash I can get my hands on. When I'd been eighteen, naive and alone, I'd blindly trusted the stranger who'd rescued me. I might have to trust him now, too, but it won't be blindly.

Making my way to check-in, I fumble through using the kiosk and then make a beeline to security. A few minutes later I'm on the other side of the metal detectors, and I stop at a store to buy random things I might need. All is going well until I arrive at my gate and hear my new name paged from the desk.

"I'm so sorry, Ms. Bensen," the fortysomething gate agent begins. "We had an administrative error, and seats were double-booked. We—"

"I have to be on this flight," I say in a whispered hiss, my heart in my throat. "I *have* to be on this flight."

"I can get you a voucher and the first flight tomorrow."

"No. Tonight. Give someone else a bigger voucher to get me a seat."

"I—"

"Talk to a supervisor," I insist. Avoiding attention means I'm usually not a pushy person, but I have no death wish. I am alive, and plan to stay that way.

She purses her lips, but finally she turns away and makes a path toward a man in uniform. Their heads dip low and he glances at me before the woman returns. "We have you on standby, and we'll try to get you on."

"How likely is it you'll get me on?"

"We're going to try."

"Try how hard?"

Her lips purse again. "Very."

I let out a sigh of relief. "Thank you. And I'm sorry. I have a . . . crisis of sorts. I really have to get to my destination." There is a thread of desperation to my voice that I can't contain.

Her expression softens. "I understand, and I am sorry this happened," she assures me. "We are trying to make this right. And so you don't panic, please know that we have to get everyone boarded before we make any passenger changes. You'll likely be the last on the plane."

"Thanks," I say, feeling awkward. "I'll just go wait." Flustered, I turn away from the counter and head to the window, where I set my bags on the floor beside me. Leaning back against the steel handrail on the glass, I position myself to see everyone around me to be sure I'm prepared for any problem before it's upon me. And that's when the room falls away, when my gaze collides with his.

He's sitting in a seat facing me, one row between us, his features handsomely carved, his dark hair a thick, rumpled finger temptation. He's dressed in faded jeans and a dark blue T-shirt, but he could just as easily be wearing a finely fitted suit and tie. He's older than me, maybe thirty, but there's a worldliness, a sense of control and confidence, about him that reaches beyond years. He is money, power, and sex, and while I cannot make out the color of his eyes, I don't need to. All that matters is that he is one hundred percent focused on me, and me on him. A moment ago I was alone in a crowd, and suddenly, I'm with him. As if the space between us is nothing. I tell myself to look away, that everyone is a potential threat, but I just . . . can't.

His eyes narrow the tiniest bit, and then his lips curve ever so slightly and I'm certain I see satisfaction slide over his face. He knows I can't look away. I've become his newest conquest, of which I am certain he has many, and embarrassingly, I've done so without one single moan of pleasure in the process.

"Inviting our first-class guests to board now," the gate agent says over the intercom.

I blink as he pushes himself to his feet and slides the strap of his duffel bag onto his shoulder. His eyes hold mine, a hint of something in them I can't quite make out. Challenge? But what kind of challenge? He turns away, and just like that, I'm alone again.

TWO

EVERYONE HAS BOARDED THE PLANE BUT me. I'm alone in the gate area aside from a few airline personnel, and I feel vulnerable and exposed with no crowd to hide me. I'm already thinking through my options for the evening if I don't make this flight, when my new name is called.

"Your lucky day, Ms. Bensen," the agent says as I approach the counter. "You've been bumped up to first class."

I blink in surprise, and not just at the oddity of being called Ms. Bensen. "Are you sure? First class?"

"That's right."

"How much extra?" I ask, unsure of how much money I have on the card I've been given, and unable to use my personal savings for fear of being tracked. I'm not even sure the little bit my extra holiday jobs allowed me would cover it.

"No cost to you," she assures me, smiling and motioning to my ticket. "I'll just print out your new boarding pass."

"Thank you," I say quickly.

As I rush down the Jetway to the plane, and despite my relief at scoring a seat, the reality of leaving New York punches me in the gut. Everything I've come to know as my world is here, and I haven't felt this helpless since . . . a long time ago.

I can't think about what happened then. I *don't* think about it. That's when the nightmares start, and so does the fear. This isn't the time to let the terror control me. I have no idea what I'll face in the next few days.

"Welcome aboard," a flight attendant says cheerfully as I reach the plane, and somehow I muster a half-smile before making my way to Row 7, where there are only two seats.

My aisle seat is empty—even though they told me the flight was overbooked—and the one by the window is empty, too. The hope that I might be alone is dashed when I note a bag stored beneath the seat. I sigh. I just want to slip into my seat and shut my eyes before whoever it is returns, but that's not an option. I have luggage to store and a file to study.

With a shrug, I let the oversized tote bag fall into my seat. When I try to stow my carry-on suitcase, I discover the bin above me is full. Apparently nothing is going to be easy tonight. Pushing myself to tiptoe, I try to adjust some bags to make room for mine, and it's as much a struggle as breathing is right now.

"Let me help you."

The deep, slightly husky male voice has me turning to my left, and I'm captured in a familiar stare. My heart sputters. It can't be. But it is. I made a fool of myself by gaping at a gorgeous man, and now I'm going to pay in buckets of embarrassment. The man from the gate area towers over my five feet three inches by close to a foot, and standing so close that I no longer have to guess the color of his eyes. They are blue, a piercing aqua blue that's almost green, and they are once again focused one hundred percent on me.

"I . . . ah . . . Thank you."

"My pleasure," he says with a quirk to his mouth that, along with the dark stubble shadowing his strong jaw and his barely-there goatee, makes me think *pirate*. The kind that steals a girl's senses and ravishes her body, leaving her incapable of anything but a whimper as she watches him walk out the door.

Mr. Tall, Dark, and Potentially Dangerous reaches over me into the compartment, his T-shirt stretching over a perfectly sculpted broad chest. I don't move—me, a person who believes wholeheartedly in personal space. I know I should, but I don't seem to have control over my legs, let alone anything else, tonight.

He glances down at me as he shifts the luggage. "Just this bag?" he asks, and there is heat in his eyes. Or maybe amusement. And conquest, definitely conquest, which must get old for a man like him.

The thought is enough to make me step back, probably a bit too obviously. "Yes. Thank you." He slides my small suitcase in, muscles flexing, tall torso stretching deliciously, and I don't even try to look away. Admiring him keeps me from thinking about the hundreds of other people on this flight who could be trouble.

"We're all set," he says, motioning to the seat. "You want the window?"

"Window?" My belly tightens and I feel breathless. "We're seated together?"

"Appears that way." Humor lights his eyes, and his mouth quirks again as he adds, "Small world."

My cheeks heat at the reference to our little encounter in the terminal. "Too small," I say.

An announcement over the intercom urges us to sit, saving me from some witty comment I don't have.

"Last chance," he says. "Window?"

About to decline, I realize that an aisle seat exposes me to all the other passengers behind me. The only person who will ravish me while I'm trapped between this man and the wall is this man. " Do you mind?"

"Not at all."

"Thank you." I grab my tote bag and move to the window seat. "Do you want your things from under the seat?"

He slides in beside me, and he is big and broad and too good-looking for the safety of womankind. "Why don't I just put yours under my seat?" he suggests.

He smells spicy and masculine, and the scent stirs a distant memory. I shove it away, frustrated that I'm back to every little thing triggering flashbacks. Today has undone the strength I'd spent years creating in myself, made me weak as I once was.

"Okay," I agree. "I'll just grab a few things for the flight." I quickly remove my file folder and my purse and hand over the tote bag, my hand brushing his. A jolt of electricity darts up my arm and I quickly turn away, buckling myself in. Maybe being locked in a corner with a man I'm powerless to control my reactions to isn't so smart.

"Champagne?"

I glance up to find a pretty twentysomething flight attendant holding a tray, looking at my seat partner with unabashed approval that makes me think of the bold way Chloe lives her life. And suddenly it's hard to breathe. I will never see Chloe again.

"Why yes, we will," my travel partner says, accepting two glasses and turning to me, successfully dismissing the flight attendant.

I hold up a hand. "No, thank you."

"We have a designated driver."

"I'm afraid it will make me sleepy," I protest, though I'm certain the visit from my guardian angel, or handler, has ensured I won't rest well again for a very long time.

"It's a four-hour flight," he points out. "Sleepy isn't a bad thing."

Sleepy. This gorgeous, incredibly masculine man has just said "sleepy," and it seems so out of the realm of what I expect from him that he manages the impossible. I smile an honest smile and accept the glass. "I suppose it's not." I sip the sweet, bubbly beverage.

A glint of satisfaction flickers in his eyes, as if he's pleased that I've done as he wishes, before he takes my glass from me and sets both our drinks in the cupholders between us. The easy way he assumes control of my tiniest actions, and seems to enjoy doing so, should bother me. Yet somehow it only makes him more tantalizingly male.

He extends his hand. "Liam Stone."

My pulse jumps at both his ridiculously alluring name and the idea of touching him. I start to lift my hand, but hesitate with the oddest sense of this moment changing my life in some way. Pushing past the crazy thought, I press my palm to his. "Nice to meet you, Liam. I'm Amy."

His fingers close around mine and a slow, warm, tingling sensation slides up my arm. "Tell me what I did to make you smile, so I can do it again." His voice is low, gravelly, as sexy as the man who owns it. I expect him to let go of me, but his fingers seem to flex around my hand, tightening as if he doesn't want to let go. And I'm shocked at how much I, someone who avoids people I don't know well, do not want him to.

"Sleepy," I manage.

His brows furrow. "Sleepy?"

"That's what you did that made me smile. You don't seem like a man who'd say 'sleepy.'"

He arches a brow, and he's *still* holding my hand.

I should object. I should pull away. He has the experience and depth I've long avoided, and craved, in a man. All I succeed in doing is melting into my chair, like I know I could easily melt *for him*.

"Is that so?" he challenges.

"Yes. That's so."

He looks amused, and—reluctantly, it seems—releases my hand. Or maybe not reluctantly. Maybe he wasn't holding it as long as it felt like he was holding it. I fear I have no concept of what's real or not anymore.

Liam leans in close, as if he plans to share a secret, and I want him even closer. "Just what kind of man do you think I am, Amy?"

The kind that flirts with lost little girls who don't even know their own names and then darts off to travel the world with a supermodel, I think, but I say, "Not the kind who says 'sleepy.'"

Laughter rumbles from his chest, the deep, masculine sound spreading warmth through my body. Impossibly, it's both fire in my veins and balm for my nerves, calming me in an inexplicable way, when I know he's too good-looking, too inquisitive, and absolutely too controlling to play with. Not that I'd even know how to play with a man like this—or any man, for that matter. Men, like friends, have been risky propositions for me.

"Why are you headed to Denver, Amy?" he asks, and the soothing balm becomes shards of glass splintering through me.

"Excuse me," the flight attendant mercifully interrupts,

saving me an answer that's still in the file I haven't read. "Can I take your dinner orders?"

"Chicken," I say.

Liam glances at me. "How do you know they have chicken?"

"It's the go-to food for hotels, parties, and airlines." And there was a time in my youth when all those things had been in my life. I glance at the flight attendant for confirmation, and she nods.

"Make that two orders of chicken," Liam says with another rumble of that powerfully addictive laughter, and while I like his easygoing nature, I can almost feel the band of control he wields over everything around him.

A muffled ringing sound fills the air and the flight attendant warns, "Whoever's phone is ringing, you have about one minute until electronic devices are off."

She moves down the aisle, and since the sound is coming from Liam's bag, I bend over to grab it, dislodging my folder from my lap in the process. My heart lurches as it tumbles to the floor and spills open, the contents flying everywhere. I grab for them, shoving papers inside the folder as quickly as I can.

"Your résumé, I believe," Liam says, and I freeze at his obvious nosy inspection of the document I have yet to read. The idea that he knows more about me than I do is unnerving. Slowly, I lift my gaze to find only a few inches separating us. His piercing eyes see too much. He makes me feel too much. I don't know him. I certainly can't trust him.

Is there anyone I can really trust left in this world?

"Thanks," I say, taking the résumé from him with more obvious snap than I intend. I tug his bag out from underneath my seat. He unzips the side pocket to remove his phone, and I'm self-conscious about how high my skirt rides up my thigh as he helps me shove the bag back where it had been.

But he isn't looking at my legs. I can feel the burn of him watching me in my cheeks. I know he knows how uncomfortable I am. I know he knows I'm not okay right now. I feel trapped. Trapped with this man, and trapped in a life that isn't mine.

Tugging at my skirt, I sit up, and he does the same, shifting his attention to his phone. Taking advantage of his distraction, I twist toward the window, giving him my back. Maybe he'll think I'm allowing him privacy for his call. Maybe he'll think I'm rude. I don't care. I open the folder, quickly find the résumé he's already seen, and start reading. Amy Bensen is, or was, a private secretary to some executive, whose name I quickly press into memory. She'd had that job since graduating college three years before, but he retired and she's been laid off.

I flip to a summary page behind the résumé that tells me my backstory and read on as Liam talks on his phone about some meeting. An announcement is made about electronic devices, and I read faster.

Amy Bensen has scored a three-month position handling the personal affairs of a private businessman who is both a friend of her ex-boss and overseas for that time period. Her new boss will be providing an apartment near his personal home, which is empty and will need to be monitored.

There's another comment on the page, typed in bold and underlined. You are not to apply for work until I contact you and tell you that it's safe. Do nothing to bring attention to yourself. I inhale a slow, heavy breath and can't seem to let it out. *Until I tell you it's safe?* What does that even mean? Who is after me? Do they, or he or she, know I was in New York? Can they figure out where I went? And why, why, *why* did I let myself pretend this threat didn't exist until I was forced into hiding again?

The plane roars to life and I nearly jump out of my skin. Casting a glance over my shoulder, I confirm that Liam didn't notice, and is concentrating on punching something into his phone. He's already started asking me questions and he'll ask more, so I have to be ready.

Thumbing through the file, I find a page with my new

family history. My mother died in a car accident four years ago, and my father was a drunk who left us when I was a kid. I have no siblings. A wave of nausea overcomes me and I shut the file. Still facing the window, I lean against the seat, squeezing my eyes shut.

I'd adored my mother. I'd worshipped my older brother. And my father would never have left me by choice. I *had* a family that was more than a typed piece of paper in a file. Now I have nothing but a fake name and a fake life.

THREE

WE LEVEL OFF AT CRUISING ALTITUDE, the soft hum of the engines lulling me into deep thought, my mind drifting to places I don't want to go. Flashes of the tattoo on my handler's wrist. The tattoo is replaced by flames. Then suddenly I'm floating in a cloud of thick smoke, trying to escape, but I can't seem to get out of it. I can't scream, though I try. But they're screaming. Oh, God. Oh, God. I have to get to them. A sudden bright light pierces the fog and I jerk to a sitting position and grab my throat, gasping for air, feeling the rasp of smoke burn through my lungs.

"Easy, sweetheart. You're okay."

I barely register the voice. I can't focus. My hands go to my face. "Where am I?"

"Amy."

Strong hands touch me, turn me, and I blink a pair of piercing aqua blue eyes into focus. Memories rush over me. "Liam?"

"Yes. Liam. That must have been one hell of a nightmare."

Nightmare? I fell asleep? "No, I . . ." Images flash in my mind, and I squeeze my eyes shut, trying to block out my fear, the smoke, the gut-wrenching screams. My fingers curl around what I realize is Liam's shirt, and on some level I know that I'm clinging to a man I barely know, but he's all I have. He's all that's keeping me from melting down.

"Amy," Liam whispers, stroking a hand over my hair.

I tell myself it's inappropriate for him to touch me like this. It's also exactly what I need, and somehow, so is he. I tell myself it's simply that he's in the right place at this very wrong time in my life—but that does nothing to discourage my reaction to his touch, to the warmth radiating from the place where my palms rest on his chest and up my arms. Without a conscious decision, I lean closer to him and my lashes lift, my eyes meeting his, and the connection shoots adrenaline through me. I am no longer in the hell of my head. I am right here with this man, and he leaves no room for anything else.

"Is she okay?"

I jerk back at the sound of the flight attendant's voice, and Liam's hands fall away from me, leaving me oddly cold. "Am I okay?" I ask, wondering what the heck I did that would merit that question.

"She doesn't like it when I talk sports," Liam jokes, obviously trying to spare me a more personal explanation of . . . what? What the heck did I do?

"Too much basketball makes me crazy," I add, trying to snatch up the breadcrumbs Liam has tossed my way, but I fear I sound too strained to sound anything other than baffled.

"It's not basketball season," she points out, looking less than pleased.

"Since when does that stop a basketball fan from killing us with basketball talk?" I ask, and that earns me a deadpan look, which has me quickly shifting gears, trying to make blind amends. "I'm fine. Sorry if I caused some kind of trouble."

She frowns and glowers accusingly at Liam, and all signs of her early admiration of his overwhelming hotness from earlier are gone. "She doesn't seem fine." Her gaze shifts to me. "You screamed. It scared the heck out of us."

Screamed? *Way to not bring attention to yourself, Amy.* "I took a decongestant," I say, trying to be convincing. "They make me sleepy and give me nightmares."

Her expression softens. "Boy oh boy, they really worked you over. We've only been in the air fifteen minutes. You were knocked out hard and fast."

Which isn't like me. Especially not on a day when I feel threatened. "I'm sorry I scared you," I offer, attempting a smile but failing. "I promise to stay awake the rest of the flight."

"Don't worry about that." She grins. "But maybe warn us before you go to sleep. We'll have dinner served in five minutes," she says, and leaves.

"Decongestants?" Liam asks softly, drawing my gaze back to his.

"My ears pop when I fly." The lie comes easily; I'm back to the me I hate. "And unless you want to confess to drugging me, that's my story and I'm sticking to it."

He studies me a bit too carefully, and something in his eyes has me warm all over and wishing he'd touch me again. "What are you afraid of, Amy?"

You, I want to say. *You make me want to trust you.* I laugh, and it sounds strained. "Godzilla." The fictional monster I'd feared in childhood, until life had shown me real monsters existed.

If I'd expected his laughter, he doesn't give it to me. "Godzilla?" he prods, angling himself to block out anyone passing by us, his body almost caging mine.

The impact of this man's full attention is overwhelming. My breath turns shallow, and to my utter disbelief, my nipples are tight and achy. I do *not* respond to men like this. I just . . . don't.

"Everyone has a proverbial monster under the bed," I manage, and thankfully my voice sounds far more steady than I feel. "And hey—at least there weren't any hippos crossing the road in this nightmare. I've had that one a couple of times. Though actually, I don't think the hippos were nightmares—just strange dreams."

Shut up, Amy, *shut up*! Why are you telling him more than you have to? You *never, ever* tell anyone more than you have to.

"I won't try to analyze what the hippos mean," he comments, and the slight curve to his lips fades as he adds, "But your monster under the bed sounds more like a skeleton in the closet to me."

"Fear and a secret are two different things," I remind him.

"They often come together. A secret that leads to fear in some shape or form."

Tension coils in my muscles. My nightmare has turned into an open window to my soul that I desperately want to slam shut. I quickly pull my guard into place and turn the tables. "You sound like a man who speaks from experience."

"Yes, well," he says, a cynical tinge to his voice, "experience isn't all it's cracked up to be, is it?"

I search his eyes for the meaning behind his words, but I find nothing. He is unreadable, as guarded as I am on my best day, and I sense that I've glimpsed a little piece of *his* soul. "What makes you have nightmares, Liam?"

"Nothing." His answer is short and fast, his tone as unreadable as his face remains.

"Everyone has something that scares them."

"I own my fear. It doesn't own me."

A sound of disbelief slips from my throat. "You make it sound so easy to control fear." I instantly regret the admission of my fear. It's a mistake I never make, but I've made it with him. Liam truly *is* dangerous.

His gaze lowers to my mouth, lingering there and sending a tingling sensation down my neck and over my breasts, before slowly lifting. "Maybe you haven't had the right teacher, Amy."

What does that even mean, and why does it create an acute throbbing between my legs? I'm spiraling out of control, and my defenses bristle. "I didn't say I needed a teacher."

"You didn't say you didn't, either."

"Dinner is served," the flight attendant announces, and neither of us looks at her.

"I don't," I say, not sure if I'm trying to convince him or me. My heart is racing. *Why* is my heart racing?

His lips twitch. "If you say so."

"Dinner is served," the flight attendant repeats, a little louder.

"I do say so," I assure him, cutting my gaze away and lowering my tray table to have my chicken dinner immediately placed on it.

The flight attendant leaves and I don't look at Liam. I have the sense that if I do, he'll see more of me than I do myself. As it is, I'm letting him see things I shouldn't have. This banter between us has to stop. It *will* stop. I'm done playing friendly seatmate.

There's a reason I stay away from men like Liam, men with experience and confidence. Men who make a girl who already can't remember her name forget her name. They *do* see too much. And they make you see too little.

I snatch up the roll I don't want and tear it apart, then set it back down. *Teacher.* What does that even mean? And why am I making myself crazy wondering, anyway? It doesn't matter. He'll be out of my life in a few short hours.

Yet the next few minutes feel like an eternity. I tell myself the silence is good. We don't have to talk, and it's better this way. Talking means giving away facts I need to suppress. It's logical; it's right. But I'm so ultra-aware of Liam beside me that I can barely taste the few bites of food I force down. Any woman would be. He's gorgeous, like a fine work of art. That's all it is.

"You didn't tell me why you're going to Denver."

My fork freezes in the rice I'd been pushing around. In a few seconds flat I go from relief that he's broken the silence to panic about sharing my new lies. I'm not ready. I don't ever *want* to be ready.

I give him a sideways look and my pulse leaps when I find him watching me. Rattled at how easily he draws a re-action from me, I'm almost snappy as I counter, "Why are *you* headed to Denver?" And darn it, there's a tiny quaver to my voice I hope he doesn't hear.

"So that's how it is, is it?"

My brow furrows and I set my fork down. "What does that mean?"

"You give what you get," he replies, and there's no mis-taking the challenge etched in his words.

No, I think. That's not how it is. That's not how it has ever been. Not in my world.

"Wouldn't life be better if that's how it truly was?" An-other quaver ripples in the depths of my question. I really need to stop talking.

This time he sets *his* fork down, turning to face me more fully. "You do know that for a 'give what you get' philosophy to work, someone has to give first, right?" And the way he looks at me, and says the words, is somehow as intimately inappropriate as when he touched me.

"And you want that to be me," I state, intentionally leaving off the question mark. I try to leave out the breathless quality of my voice, too, but I fail. Another sign that I have no control over myself. Worse, I think I might like it if this virtual stranger had control over me—which tells me how emotionally on edge I really am.

"I'm in discussions to be part of a downtown Denver building project," he surprises me by saying. Giving before he gets.

"What kind of building project?"

He just looks at me, and I cave to his silent demand that I give as well. "I was laid off and my old boss got me a job in Denver. And before you ask, it's nothing exciting. It's administrative."

He tilts his head slightly. "So you'll be staying in Denver."

"For a while," I say, and the satisfaction I see in his eyes surprises and pleases me far more than it should. I ask the obvious question, telling myself it's simply because it's expected. "How long will you be in Denver?"

"It all depends on whether I take on the project."

The flight attendant proves she has brilliant timing again by choosing this moment to clear our plates, leaving me with an incomplete answer. By the time we've been offered coffee and dessert that we both decline, I have no idea if he would have said more, or how to get things back on topic without seeming too interested.

And *I am* too interested. He could be an enemy. But even if he's a mere stranger, I'm too risky for anyone to be-friend. And with that blistering thought, I know there is nothing more to ask him. Nothing more to say but "have a nice life." I can't ever be close to anyone. Ever.

I snuggle under the blanket the flight attendant has left for me, and Liam reaches into the seat pocket in front of my seat and removes a sketchpad I hadn't noticed before. He pauses halfway between my seat and his, glancing at me, and he is close, his mouth within leaning distance. It's a great mouth, sensual and full, and I wonder what it would feel like on mine.

"If you want to sleep," he says, "I promise to keep Godzilla at bay for you."

He couldn't have said anything more perfect, and I know right then what it is about Liam that makes him so ir-resistible. Men have been scarce in my life because of my fear of getting close to anyone. The few times I've broken that rule haven't turned out well, and in a few lonely, weak moments, I've indulged in Cinderella fantasies where my Prince Charming swoops in and makes life better. Liam is good-looking and confident, and radiates control the way my fantasy Prince Charming would. But even more, I believe Liam *would* fight Godzilla if he had to. Maybe not for me, but for someone he cares about.

"I'll hold you to that," I finally say, unable to find even a thread of jest to lace the words.

I watch his eyes flicker, the color diluting to a soft blue, then darkening again, and I have no idea how to read the meaning, since he's so guarded—as much a mystery as whoever I'm running from. "Good," he replies simply, and leans back into his seat.

Letting my head drop to the seatback, I indulge in a fantasy about Liam to keep the monsters of my past at bay. But soon the hum of the plane's engine starts working on me again, flickering images of the past begin to slip into my head, and I start to unravel. I'm not going to be able to sit here without getting lost in my own head and going crazy. A flash of flames has me jerking to a sitting position and my hands fly to my face, my elbows to my knees. I can feel the heaviness of Liam's attention. He's looking at me, but I don't want to look at him. If I do, I will talk to him. I will ask him questions. *He* will ask *me* questions.

"Amy?"

His voice slides through me, and somehow manages to be soothing, warm comfort and sensual fire at the same time. I'm baffled again by the way he manages to be silk on my raw nerves, but I'm not going to overanalyze it. I have to hold myself together until I'm someplace safe enough to cave to a little temporary weakness, and he feels like the answer. He's what will get me through this flight.

I sit back up to look at him, and my heart races as I take in his dark good looks and piercing blue eyes.

He sets his pencil down and abandons his work for me, giving me a concerned once-over. "Everything okay?" he asks, and I think of him as a gentle lion in that moment, only it is me who is purring under his powerful male attention.

"Fine," I reply, because "fine" is nothing but a word. There's no agreement on my end, no lie. I tilt my head back. Liam closes his tray and does the same, sticking his pad between his seat and the armrest.

Heads on our headrests, we stare at each other, and for several moments I'm lost in the deep blue pools of his eyes. "You do know," he says slowly, "that as a man, I've been taught that a woman never means 'fine' when she says 'fine,' right?"

I might have smiled another day, but not this one. "I guess we all have our own ways of defining *fine*."

He continues to study me as if he's trying to understand me, and I wish him good luck. I don't even understand me. "You don't want to sleep," he says.

Dodge and weave, I tell myself. "I don't like to sleep in public places."

"Talk to me, Amy," he murmurs softly.

I want to talk to him. That's the problem.

He continues, "You need to fill the empty space in your head, and right now, talking is your only method of doing that."

I try to joke away his suggestion. "And you'd rather talk to a stranger than have her fall asleep and get you in trouble with the flight attendant again, right?"

"We aren't strangers anymore, and I find the idea of occupying your time increasingly appealing." His eyes light up. "So use me, baby."

The air crackles between us and there is no denying the growing attraction I have to this man. "Fine, then. I'd love to hear about the project you're traveling to Denver to discuss."

"There isn't a lot to tell yet. It's a typical property development deal. A group of deep pockets get together and aspire to greatness that equates to dollar signs in their eyes. In this case, it's a plan to create the world's largest event center, complete with concert facilities, a shopping mall, and an office complex."

He sounds blasé, when I'm excited just hearing about the project and I find I'm more curious about Liam than ever—enough to be nosy. "Are you one of those deep pockets?"

"There are too many egos fighting in one room for me on this one. Egos translate to delays and problems."

He didn't deny he has deep pockets. I was right. He *is* money, sex, and power. "So then, what's your role, if not as an investor?"

"I'm the architect they want to design the project."

I sit up straighter at this surprising news. "You're an architect?"

"Yes."

"An architect that could create a project of the magnitude you just described?"

"Yes."

"Would I know any of your work?"

"I've done a few high-profile projects."

I frown. "Isn't this where you drop names and impress me?"

"Do I need to impress you?"

My cheeks heat. "No. I . . . most people . . ."

"I'm not most people."

No. No, he most definitely is not most people. "Have you thought about your design for this project?"

"I've drafted my vision, but I already know it's not likely to please the financiers."

"But they requested you. They must like your work."

"They want me to create the tallest building in the United States."

I blink. "Could you really do that?"

"'Can I' isn't the question. 'Will I' is the question. Height is a short man's dream of perfection. It's also narrow-minded. How high you stand isn't as important as how magnificent you are."

Magnificent. The word resonates deeply for me. I'd once thought I'd be a part of something I could describe that way. "Are you allowed to show me your design?"

"I'm allowed to do whatever the hell I want." He reaches for his sketchpad and thumbs through it to open it to a particular drawing, and starts to hand it to me, but pulls back. "I don't normally show my work to anyone until it's complete."

"But you're going to show me?"

"Yes, Amy. I'm going to show you."

He offers me the pad and I accept it, but my attention remains on him. "Why would you show me what you show no one else?"

"Because I want to."

"Thank you." Touched and confused, I look at the drawing and shock radiates through me, trapping air in my lungs. I blink, certain I'm not seeing what I am seeing, but the image remains the same. He showed me what he shows no one else, and what he has shown me is a piece of my past. That can mean only one thing. Adrenaline courses through me and I shove the pad between the cushion and wall beside me, then reach for his right arm and turn his wrist faceup, searching for the tattoo that would tell me if he's my handler.

FOUR

HIS WRIST IS BARE, AND I grab the other one; maybe my memory of which arm had the tattoo is wrong. But there is nothing. No tattoo. No proof that he's a part of my past or my future. My eyes lift to his and he arches a brow. "Problem?"

"You don't have a tattoo?"

His lips curve and his eyes light with mischief and heat. "Not that I can show you on the plane."

I ignore the implication and search for what lies beneath his amusement, but I find nothing. No secrets. No hidden agenda. But if he expected my reaction to the drawing, why would he react any other way? Then again, I could simply be losing my mind.

I drop his hand and lift the sketchpad again, staring at the drawing of a high-rise framed by a pyramid. It's *just a* pyramid. There's no code in the center. It's not tall and narrow, like the one on my note. It doesn't really resemble the tattoo at all. Maybe it *is* just a building design. Maybe it has nothing to do with me or my father.

Liam leans in, his arm brushing mine, sending a jolt of awareness through me. "My inspiration came from the two years I spent in Egypt, working with a team of experts who studied the Great Pyramid."

Impossibly, my skeletons have jumped out of the closet and attacked him, and he's not even questioning my bizarre actions. Confused, I turn to look at him. "You aren't going to ask why I just . . . did what I did?"

"No. I'm not going to ask."

"Why?"

"You'll tell me when you're ready."

"I'm not going to be ready before this plane lands."

"That's fine." He lifts a chin at the sketchpad. "You haven't said what you think of my vision."

He's confusing me. Okay, *everything* is confusing me. But

his question is an escape, and I take it. "The design is what you said you wanted it to be. It's magnificent."

"You aren't even looking at it."

"No. I'm looking at you. The man who created it." The man who wanted me to see what he wouldn't show anyone else.

"And what do you see, looking at me, Amy?"

"What you let me see."

He looks intrigued by that answer, maybe even pleased. "Ask me what I see when I look at you."

More than I want him to. "No. I don't want to know what you see." I turn away from him, sinking low in my seat and pulling the blanket to my chin, clear on only one thing: I don't like who I've become.

"WAKE UP, AMY." I blink at the feel of a hand on my shoulder and turn to find Liam leaning over me, his mouth impossibly close to mine.

"I was asleep again?"

"Like a rock."

"Please tell me I didn't scream."

"No. We're about to—"

The wheels hit the runway with a hard bump, and I'm shocked to realize that I've slept so deeply. It's as if my mind just shut down.

"I didn't want the landing to scare you," Liam explains, settling back in his seat.

"Thank you. It would have." I sit up, adjusting my skirt and folding the blanket.

"What's your plan from here?"

"Plan?"

"Do you have a ride to wherever you're going?"

"A . . . a friend is picking me up," I lie. He wants this to continue, and so do I, but I don't know his real motivation, nor I can risk his safety by being seen with him.

"Male or female?"

I blink back to the present. "What?"

"Your friend picking you up. Male or female?"

I know the safe answer is "male." If his motivation for asking is simple male interest, it will discourage him. Yet I hear myself say, "Female."

His eyes darken, and I think he's pleased with my answer. "I'll help you with your bags."

"No, I—"

"I'm helping you with your bags, Amy."

There is command in his voice and I am instantly, unbelievably aroused, and pleased at his insistence when I should be running for the hills. I *will* run for the hills when the doors open. "Thank you," I murmur and turn away from him, afraid he will read my intention in my face. I make sure my folder and bag are intact, slide the leather strap over my shoulder, and I'm ready for action.

The plane parks at the gate, and Liam retrieves my bag from the overhead compartment. Once he hands it to me, I lift the handle and tell myself to make my escape, but I'm frozen in regret over leaving him.

Too soon, he jerks his bag free and I'm out of time. Then a man moves between us and I take the opportunity to dart for the exit. I don't look back, though I want to.

A few minutes later, I'm outside in a long cab line with no cabs in sight. Thanks to several conventions and some Hollywood event, it appears I have plenty of time to savor my regret over leaving Liam behind. And I do. I savor it like I would water in a desert.

As I'm contemplating how good he might have tasted, a black Town Car stops directly beside me. The door opens and, to my shock, Liam steps out and grabs my bag.

"Come with me," he orders, not giving me time to argue. He's already at the trunk, where the driver sets my bag inside. I consider leaving it behind and running. I *should* leave it and run.

I charge toward him and meet him at the back door. My chin lifts, and he is taller than I realized, and his sleek goatee is impossibly sexy, nearly distracting me from my anger. "You can't just take my bag and demand I come with you."

"And yet that's exactly what I did. Get in the car, Amy."

I bristle at the command. "I don't know you."

His piercing blue eyes darken. "I have every intention of remedying that."

A thrill shoots through me at the obvious promise that he will be my lover, and there's no denying that I'm seduced by his confidence and dark good looks. By the gentle lion I believe will take control of everything around him, including me. He'll demand much of me, and perhaps take more than I should give. Yet beyond all reason, I want to experience those things. I want to experience him. It almost feels . . . necessary.

A cab honks at our driver. Though I have nothing to go on, instinct tells me I can trust Liam, and it has never failed me. Even when I took the museum job—my instinct told me that it was a mistake. The horn blasts again, and I go with my gut. I get in the car. Liam follows me inside and shuts the door.

"Where are we going?" the driver calls over his shoulder, pulling away from the curb.

I quickly slide my tote bag to the seat between Liam

and me, and I'm suddenly too nervous to look at him. He's experienced in ways I can't even pretend to be, worldly in ways I once thought I'd be.

Opening the folder from my handler, I read out my new address, trusting this man at a time when it's the last thing I should be doing.

"I approve," Liam says as I put the folder in my leather tote.

"Approve?" I ask, aware of him on every level. His size. His spicy scent. The burn of anger over my leaving him behind in the depth of his stare, which hasn't quite faded.

"The location your new boss picked for you. It's a safe area."

I seize the opportunity to learn more about this man for whom I am risking so much—perhaps too much. "You know Denver that well?"

"Yes. I know Denver quite well."

"Did you design another building here?"

"The tallest one downtown."

"I thought you weren't into the whole 'bigger is better' thing."

"It was a notch on the proverbial bedpost of a young architect."

I can't help but wonder if I'm setting myself up to be a notch on his proverbial bedpost, as well. "You're still young."

"I started young, so I'm younger than one would think a seasoned architect might be."

"When you say 'started young,' that means what?"

"I was an apprentice to a very famous architect from the time I was thirteen until his death four years ago."

"Thirteen? You started your career at thirteen?"

"I started my training at thirteen." He lowers his voice. "You do know I couldn't let you run, don't you?"

"I wasn't—"

"You were."

"If you think that, then why did you come after me?"

"Because you didn't want to run. You just thought you had to."

"That's a little arrogant."

"It's honest. I like honesty."

I like it, too, but I can't give it to him. This ride was a mistake. "Liam—"

He closes the distance between us, moving my bag out of the way, his powerful leg pressed to mine, his fingers sliding into my hair. I am shocked. I am excited and scared, frozen and burning up at the same time.

"Do you know how much I like it when you say my name?" he asks, his voice a soft, seductive purr.

Nerves and heat collide like fire in my belly. This man who is overwhelmingly male, a powerful force like none I have ever experienced, likes it when I say his name? "I don't know what to say to that." It is as honest an answer as I've given anyone in years.

"You don't have to know, Amy. It's okay not to know."

For the second time today, he has spoken words straight to my soul. Relief that reaches far beyond this moment flows through me. *This* is why I'm in this car, why I am drawn to this man. He makes me feel like I don't have to hold up the world on my own. As crazy as it is, from the moment my eyes met his in the terminal, he's made me feel that I'm not alone.

His thumb runs over my bottom lip, and a shiver trickles down my spine. I think he will kiss me. I want him to kiss me. But he doesn't.

"Soon," he promises, as if he knows how much I crave his mouth on mine. His cell phone rings as he adds, "And not soon enough."

He moves away from me and I want to pull him back. I want to feel his hands on my body again, his leg pressed to mine. But he's already answering his call, too easily dismissing what I cannot. "Yes," he says to his caller. "I'm here."

My fingers curl, nails digging into my palm. I have no one who'll call and ask if *I'm* here. I have only me. And no matter how drawn I am to Liam, there can *only* be me.

But as I glance at his strong profile, I briefly pretend that he is truly with me, and that I am truly with him. It's a small dream in the middle of a nightmare.

THIRTY MINUTES AFTER we leave the airport, the Town Car pulls to a stop. Liam grabs my tote bag and exits curbside while the driver opens my door. I step out, enjoying a cool evening breeze that drives home the fact that I'm no longer in New York. The street is lined with high-end restaurants and stores and, despite it being nearly midnight, people are casually strolling along the sidewalks.

With my apartment key in my hand, I glance behind me to find more stores and a hotel, and then forward, where apartment balconies rise above the retail stores.

"Hang onto my bags," I hear Liam tell the driver, before he joins me, my small suitcase and leather tote in tow. "What apartment number?"

"222, but I don't see an entrance."

"The driver said there's an elevator entrance beside the kitchen store."

Spotting the Sur La Table he must be talking about, I turn to him and reach for my suitcase. "Thanks for the ride."

He holds on to both of my bags. "You're alone in a new city. I'm not letting you go inside an apartment you've never seen before by yourself."

"The driver—"

"Has been tipped well." He motions me forward and starts walking, effectively giving me no room to argue.

Staring after him, I am on unsteady ground, inexperienced with a man as dominant and stubborn as he is. I didn't think this part of the evening through when I accepted the ride. I have no idea what awaits me at the apartment. What if there's something I can't let Liam see?

Double-stepping in my high heels, and not all that gracefully, I catch up to him. "You really don't have to—"

He cuts me a sideways look. "Right. I don't have to. You don't have to. But we are, baby, and we both know it."

My heart sputters at the obviously naughty sexual reference. "I was talking about walking me to the door. You don't have to walk me to the door."

He shoots me an evil smile. "I wasn't."

"Liam—"

"Amy." We stop at an outdoor elevator and he punches the button, amusement dancing in his eyes. "When do you start work?"

The elevator dings and opens. "I don't know." I enter the car, trying to think of an answer that isn't a lie.

He steps in beside me and punches the button. "You don't know?"

"I'm supposed to get settled first."

He scowls, and even his scowl is handsome. "How well do you know your new employer?"

Now I scowl. "How well does anyone know their employer?"

"You moved here for this person."

"A job is not a person, and I know just as much about him as I do you." The elevator opens again and I don't give him time for a rebuttal. I step into a carpeted hallway that reminds me of a hotel corridor and note the sign pointing me to my right.

"Your boss didn't make sure you got here safely tonight," he points out as he joins me, and we make our way to the last apartment at the end of the hallway. "I did. Do you have your key?"

I hold it up between two fingers and stop in front of the assigned door. I just can't think of it as "my door." "I'm all set."

"I'm coming in to make sure you're safe."

"This is good," I assure him quickly.

"You have no idea what's waiting for you inside."

Exactly. "An empty apartment. And I don't know you, Liam. I can't invite you inside." I have no idea what makes me say it, but I add, "Not tonight."

"That's better than not ever," he comments. "But I'm not a serial killer, and for all I know, your new boss is. Let me check the place out for you. You can stay outside while I do."

"I'm not letting you in."

He leans in close and presses his hand on the door above me. I can feel the heat rushing off his body, and I can almost taste the masculine scent of him. Or maybe I just want to taste *him*.

"I'm going to get a room across the street," he informs me.

"Your hotel is across the street?"

"It is now. I'll be back in fifteen minutes with a list of restaurants open at this time of the night we can choose from. My name is Liam Stone, Amy. Look me up on your computer. Then you'll know I'm trustworthy."

"I don't have a computer."

"Or enough clothes to be moving from state to state."

I left myself wide open for that one. "I had them shipped along with my other things."

He doesn't look convinced. "Right. Look me up. Use your cell phone."

"It's broken. I have to get a new one tomorrow."

"It's broken." His tone is flat.

"Yes. It's broken."

53

He considers me a moment. "Stay here, and don't go inside yet." Without further explanation, he walks toward the elevator.

Confused, I open my mouth to call after him, but snap it shut. It's midnight. People are sleeping. He steps into the elevator and, regardless of what he's planning, I know he'll be back—which means I need to act fast. I unlock the door, flip on the light, and tug my suitcase and bag along with me.

A small hallway leads past a kitchen to my left and directly into a large, open dining and living area. Thankfully, I have furniture, which is more than I had when I was sent to New York. I scan the overstuffed brown couch and two chairs, then spot an envelope on the simple wooden dining table. I set my bag down and sink into one of the wooden chairs that match the table, and reach for the envelope.

The contents are disappointingly uninformative. There's only a lease for the apartment, with a note telling me to sign it and drop it by the real estate agent's office. The first month's rent is paid.

Nothing else. No information about what has happened. No explanation of the threat I might be under. No triangle symbol—it's nowhere to be seen. My heart starts to race. There's supposed to be a symbol on any instructions I get. Maybe he considered this note an extension of the last, so it didn't need it?

I don't know what this means. I can't think. I have to get rid of Liam and go to an ATM to see how much money I have to live on. Should I run? I don't know. I just don't *know*.

I have to take one thing at a time. Liam first. The rest later.

Shoving away from the table, I rush back to the door and open it, gasping when I find Liam standing there, dark blue T-shirt stretched over his impressive chest. And he doesn't look happy.

"I told you not to go inside. It wasn't safe."

Having him, or anyone, worry about me feels so good, I don't bristle at his reprimand. "Well, as you see, I did go inside, and I'm happy to report that Godzilla is nowhere in sight."

He doesn't look any more pleased than moments before. "We'll talk about that later."

My brows dip. I'm not sure I'm processing content properly right now. Why wasn't the symbol on the note? "Talk about what?"

"Later," he repeats tightly, and hands me an iPad. "My Wikipedia page is up. Look it over. There's a hotel directly across the street. I'll get a room and suggestions for places to eat that will still be open."

My eyes go wide. "You have a Wikipedia page?"

"Yes. I have a Wikipedia page, and despite the unauthorized information it contains, it's fairly accurate. I'm going to check into my hotel. I'll be back to get you in a few." He starts to turn away.

"Liam, wait." He pauses and looks at me. "I don't have a Wikipedia page. I'm no one special."

"You're you. That's what counts." He turns and leaves.

You're you. Only that's the whole problem. I'm *not* me.

FIVE

PER WIKIPEDIA, LIAM STONE IS A reclusive billionaire and philanthropist who lost both of his parents at a young age and was taken in by one of the most famous architects who ever lived. Liam inherited his mentor's extreme wealth and, apparently, also had his skill. At only thirty-one, Liam is the highest-paid living architect in the world and is considered an architectural prodigy.

Setting the iPad aside, I press my fingers to my throbbing temples. It's almost comical that I actually thought Liam could be my handler. He has far more to occupy himself with than me, and I really don't know why he's hovering around me at this point. Well, unless he just wants to have sex. It's certainly on my mind, and maybe I should just have a one-night stand and let Liam take me away for a few hours. Whatever awaits me will still be there tomorrow. It might even stop me from melting down.

So why do I feel so let down that this thing with him isn't more? I can't have more. I went into the apartment to get rid of him, and when he comes back I should pretend I'm not here.

But when a knock sounds I jump to my feet and rush to open the door, nearly swallowing my tongue with the impact he has on me. The man does a pair of faded Levi's and a T-shirt as right as they can be done. And he does it while looking at me like I'm dinner and he's going to lick me off the plate.

"Done with your research?" he queries.

"Yes. I read your Wikipedia page."

"And?"

"You're rich, talented, and why are you at my door again?" *And why am I not sending you away?*

"Because you haven't invited me in."

"You sure don't seem like a recluse to me."

His lips quirk and before I can blink he's advanced on

me, his hands coming down on my shoulders, his big body crowding into the apartment.

"Liam," I object. Sort of. Actually, I'm not sure I object at all.

"Amy," he counters.

My nerves prickle. "Don't do that."

He closes the door, pressing me against the wall, his powerful thighs encasing mine. "Do what, baby?"

The endearment does funny things to my stomach, and so does the solid wall of his chest beneath my fingers. "Mock me when I say your name."

"I assure you, I'm not mocking you. I told you how hot it makes me when you say my name."

I'm *so* not skilled at this flirtatious word game he's playing, so I resort to what I do well. "I didn't invite you in."

"No?" he asks, his eyes alight with amusement.

"No." And while I'm out of my league with a man this experienced and incredibly sexy, his playfulness takes the edge off.

"Well," he says, his voice holding a hint of mischief, "I prefer privacy when I kiss you. We recluses are like that."

My nerves shoot to the sky. He wants to kiss me. I *want* him to kiss me. "You're no recluse," I accuse, wondering how Wikipedia got that so very wrong.

His eyes darken, narrow. "Then how would you describe me, Amy?" he asks, and again his voice is low, gravelly. Affected by me. The idea is exciting and frightening.

"Demanding," I say, as breathlessly as I feel.

His fingers curve around my neck, tugging my mouth near his, teasing me with the promise of a kiss. "You have no idea just how demanding I can be." And with that erotic promise, his tongue slices into my mouth, a silky, hot caress that seems to touch every inch of my tingling body. The taste of him, of hot passion and desire, sizzles through my senses, and my fingers splay on the hard wall of his chest.

A soft groan escapes him and his hand caresses my backside, pulling my hip against his, his thick erection pressing into my belly. "I've wanted to taste you since the moment I saw you in the terminal," he murmurs, his breath a warm, wicked seduction against my mouth.

"Feel free to do it again," I whisper, with unusual boldness. But then, I've never had anyone as tantalizing as him to inspire me.

"I'm going to do a whole lot more than kiss you, baby," he promises, and his mouth covers mine, his tongue once again pressing past my lips, and I feel the lick between my thighs, in the deep throb of my sex. I've never felt desire like this, and I like it far too much to let anything interfere. *This one night is for me*, I think—and the thought is liberating.

He's like no one I've ever known, and I'll probably never see him again. Determined to enjoy every minute with him, and every inch of him, I sink into the kiss, my tongue caressing his, drinking him in. I slip my hands under his shirt, feeling hard muscle beneath warm, taut skin. Touching him is wonderful, addictive, making me tremble inside.

Confidence builds inside me, and my hand strokes a path down his zipper. His hand goes to mine and he pulls his mouth away, his fingers move from my neck, tangling in my hair, tugging me backward with a gentle, erotic force. "How old are you?"

The question shatters a little part of me. This is *not* a re-action a girl wants when touching a man. "Why does that matter?"

"How old, Amy?"

"Twenty-four." I don't even know why I answer. I shouldn't have answered.

"How many men have you fucked?"

I gasp. "You can't ask me that."

"I just did. How many?"

I don't like where this has gone. I don't like how I suddenly don't know if he thinks I'm a virgin due to my limited experience, or a hussy for my bold actions. Either way, this is not an escape anymore.

I try to shove away from him, but his grip doesn't loosen. "Let go," I hiss. "This was a mistake. I don't know you. I don't do this kind of thing."

"It's quite clear that you don't do this kind of thing," he says, releasing me, and I hate how much I wish he hadn't, after what he's made me feel. And how relieved I am when he plants his hands by my head, caging me as if he doesn't want me to escape. "But I do, Amy. I do this kind of thing a lot. I have short, well-protected affairs with women who know I'm not going to be around tomorrow. Women who don't care enough about who I am to find out my name or how much money I have."

My defenses flare, verging on anger. Is he accusing me of being a virgin, a slut, or a money-grubber? "I didn't try to find out about you. You told me to read the Wikipedia page. You brought your iPad here with your page up."

"I know. I wanted you to know me and to trust me. I still do."

I soften, confused. I stay confused with this man. "I don't understand. You just said . . . why are you . . . I don't . . ." My God, I'm an educated woman, and I've lost the ability to form coherent sentences.

"The same reason I showed you my design on the plane."

"Which is why?"

"Because against every rule I've set, I wanted to."

"I don't know what that means."

"Then let me be more clear." His cheek slides over mine, his whiskers scraping erotically over my delicate skin, his lips pressing to my ear. "You're a beautiful woman who deserves to be properly fucked, and I conclude from your actions and your answers to my questions that you haven't been. I want to be the man to remedy that. I want it very much." His arm wraps my waist, shackling me to him as if he fears I will get away, his free hand stroking down my hair, as he huskily adds, "Probably too much." His intense blue eyes stare down at me, searching mine. "I don't know what you're running from, but I know you're running."

My heart jackhammers. "No, I'm not."

He brushes his lips over mine. "I'm not asking you to tell me why," he says, rejecting my denial. "But I have every intention of making you forget everything but what it feels like to have my tongue and my cock buried inside you."

My lashes lower and heat pools low in my belly, then settles hard between my thighs. I've never had a man use the word "fuck" with me before, let alone promise to fuck me properly—but I fear that he'll make me forget why my silence is golden. "I don't know—"

"Look at me, Amy." There's a command in his voice, and for reasons I can't explain, I'm compelled to comply. "I do," he promises. "And I want to be the man who'll make sure you do, too."

He'll make sure I know. This is exactly everything I need to hear. He's promised to be demanding and to take me to unknown territory, but he's also promising that I won't be there in the dark. I am so very tired of being in the dark.

I wrap my arms around his neck, and make sure he knows how important this is to me. "I want to know. I need to know."

Approval seeps into his eyes, passion simmering in their depths, and one of his strong hands cradles my face, and then his mouth lowers to mine. His tongue tastes me, and he's different now, we're different now. The kiss is hotter, wilder, unleashed, and I have a sense of being claimed, like I'm his to take. And I want to be taken by this man. I want it very much.

Still kissing me, as if he can't get enough of me, either, he lifts me off the floor, his hands cradling my backside. My legs wrap around his waist, and one of my shoes falls to the ground, so I kick the other one free. "Where's the bedroom?" he asks, the urgency in his voice mirroring what I feel.

"The right, I think."

He starts walking and I bury my head in his neck, inhaling his scent, and tiny splinters of memory begin to pierce the fog of desire. I shove them away, refusing to be consumed by the past when I have this man to consume me instead.

When we reach the bedroom, he curses under his breath. "No sheets, pillows, or blankets," he says, retracing his steps to the hallway. "Your boss should have made sure this was handled."

"I'm sure he didn't think—"

"Exactly. I'm taking you to my hotel, where I can lick you from head to toe on proper bedding."

"What? No." He shifts my weight and reaches for the door. "Stop!"

He straightens, and he doesn't look pleased. "Stop why?"

My mind races for an answer, one of the many lies I live to tell. "My apartment is directly across from the hotel. I'll see the staff around the neighborhood. I don't want them thinking of me as the floozy some rich guy brought to his bed for a night every time I walk by."

He arches a brow. "Rich guy? Floozy?"

"That's what it will seem like, Liam."

He scowls and lowers me to the floor, pressing me against the door, his hands settling possessively on my waist. "You aren't a floozy. You know that, right?"

I hate the excuse I've made, the lie that is my life, and the idea that it might push him out the door, that he might not ever touch me again, is unbearable enough to give me courage. "If you want to fuck me, it's here and now. Otherwise, goodnight, Liam. Thanks for the ride."

He sets his hands on his hips, no longer touching me, and I'm shaken by how much the loss of connection affects me. I'm used to being alone. I'm used to not being touched. "This is crazy, Amy. Your apartment isn't ready to be lived in."

This place is not, and never will be, my apartment. But he can't know that. "I need to stay here tonight," I say, not pleased with the way my voice cracks.

Liam notices, too. I see it in the slight flicker in his eyes. "You *need* to be here?"

"Yes." My voice is no stronger now than moments before, damn it. "I need to be here."

He leans in, one hand on the wall by my face, his big body close but still not touching me. Why do I need him to touch me this badly?

"Then I need to be here tonight," he declares. "*We* will be here tonight."

We. I know the word really means nothing. This is just one night. But I like the idea of being "we" right now. And I desperately want to get back to forgetting everything but him. I push myself to tiptoe and press my lips to his.

His arm wraps my waist again and he pulls me close, his body a warm, welcome shelter from the nightmare I've left outside this door. "I'm not going anywhere you aren't to-night," he promises.

It's enough. It has to be enough. It *will be* enough. "Good. I don't want you to."

I've barely said the words when he turns me to face the door. "What are you doing?" I demand.

He steps closer, his hips framing mine, the thick ridge of his erection pressed to my backside. "Preparing you."

"Preparing me?" I gasp. "What does that mean?"

He tugs my jacket down my shoulders, tangles it around my arms, then turns me to face him. "You can free your hands, but don't."

"No." I knew he'd ask for too much. "I can't do this. I can't—"

He cups my cheeks. "Deep breaths, baby. I know you're on unfamiliar ground, and I know you barely know me, but I'm just going to make you come. Pure pleasure, nothing more. I know that when things feel out of control, you think you need control. But sometimes, having a safe place to give it away is the best way to block everything else out. I'm asking you to let me show you I'm that safe place."

But he'll be gone tomorrow, and then where will I be? What place will my mind have traveled to, and will I get back to where I was before? "Do *you* ever give away control?"

"No. That's not what works for me."

"But you think it will work for me." I just want . . . more. More understanding. More . . . him.

"It will work for you. Let me teach you, Amy."

Teach me. This is what he'd been talking about on the plane. And this is so far into new territory, I don't know which direction to go. I crave what he'll show me, but I fear what I'll show him.

"Do you have things you need to block out, Liam?" I'm on tenterhooks, waiting on an answer that feels important to me, even though I don't even know what I expect or want it to be.

"Yeah, baby," he surprises me by saying, "I do. Knowing you need the escape and admitting it, if only to yourself, *is* control." I am surprised by his willingness to share something so personal with me. I'm beyond aroused by this man, and when his finger traces the skin at the top of my blouse, I feel the touch in every part of my body. "I know that all too well." He starts unbuttoning my blouse. "And now I'm going to show you how we escape together."

I like how that sounds, but . . .

"Right here in the hallway?" I ask as my blouse begins to gape, exposing the thin lace covering my breasts.

"Right here in the hallway." His hot gaze rakes the swell of my breasts, his deft fingers finishing the buttons and pop-ping open the front clasp of my bra. He covers my breasts with his hands, and nuzzles my neck at the same time, and the mix of eroticism and tenderness ignites my senses and soothes my nerves. "You smell like sunflowers."

"My perfume," I whisper, and unbidden, my mind goes to New York, where everything I own, and no longer have, remains.

"It's perfect," he approves, tugging my nipples, and the unexpected, bittersweet ache leaves no room for the thought of what's behind me. There's only the burn for now, for him, for the escape he has promised me. My lashes flutter, and just that quickly he's on his knees, inching my skirt upward, and I ache to feel him inside me. I'm in a haze of desire and my skirt is somehow at my waist, his tongue tracing the top of one of my thigh-highs, then traveling up and down my leg. The urge to tug my hands free, to tunnel my fingers into his thick, dark hair and force his mouth where I want it, is almost too much to bear.

"I want to touch you," I pant. "I need to touch you."

His eyes meet mine, hot with desire and dark with command. "Not yet," he orders, and with no warning, he wraps his fingers around the thin strips at my hips and tugs my panties down to my feet. Then Liam's fingers are exploring the slick, wet center of my body, and his mouth is on my upper thigh, teasing me with where it might go, and I hope it soon will.

He slips two fingers deep inside me, making me pant and moan. I'm so wet and so aroused, I'm sure I will come too quickly. I try to resist the sensations building low in my belly and blooming into my sex, but it consumes me like a black hole where nothing but pleasure exists, dragging me deep into the center of spiraling, delicious sensations. They overcome me, *he* overcomes me, and my sex clenches so intensely that I jerk and I nearly fall down.

Liam's arm wraps around me, holding me up, and his tongue slows as my muscles ease and I relax. He pulls my jacket from my wrists and I wrap my arms around him for stability and bury my face in his neck. He takes me down with him as he sits against the door, with me straddling him, and all I can think is how embarrassed I am. Did I even last one minute? Two? Please let it have been at least five.

"Amy," he murmurs. "Look at me."

"No. I can't."

"You can," he says firmly, tilting my face up to his. "Don't be embarrassed."

"I can't help it." My voice shakes; I've never felt this exposed. "I was—"

"Beautiful." His hand moves to cup my cheek. "Absolutely beautiful and sexy."

I laugh, a choked sound. "I was fast. Embarrassingly fast."

"I like that I can turn you on that easily." He caresses my shirt and bra off of my shoulders, and my mind is mush all over again. And when he tenderly kisses my shoulder, his hot stare raking over my naked torso, my breasts are instantly heavy, and my nipples tight.

His eyes lift to mine. "And I like that you like it when I look at you." His finger lightly teases my nipple, and a shiver of pure pleasure slides down my back. His lips curve. "And that you're so responsive when I touch you."

A pinching sensation begins to form in my chest. I'm emotionally overwhelmed, when I should simply be aroused. I barely know this man, yet somehow he goes deep into my soul and speaks to me like no one else ever has.

But it's just the pressure of today's events. It's not him.

I avert my gaze, trying to pull myself together, but his finger tilts my chin up, forcing my eyes back to his. "Don't hide what you feel, baby. That's the thing about fucking properly: it's raw and honest. There's no time limit or embarrassment or nerves—it's just us fucking. Us feeling. Us being us together. We leave everything else at the door." He smiles a sexy, easy smile and his hands slide up my back, his forehead resting against mine. "Don't ever be embarrassed with me."

My fingers curl on his cheek, the soft rasp of his newly formed whispers teasing my skin, my tension fading into the seductive promise of his words. "I'm trying. This is . . ." I trail off, uncertain what I was going to say, uncertain what I really feel.

"I'll help you." He drags a finger down my cheek. "The only reason I wanted to go to the hotel was that I wanted this to be good for you. And I think you need to be pampered tonight."

"I can't," I whisper, the two words—so telling, so honest—out before I can stop them.

He leans back and I'm naked beyond the absence of my blouse, exposed beneath his too-keen inspection. And I think he can see my desire to escape into his world and run from mine, if only for a little while. And I fear I have let him see too much.

Steeling myself for whatever questions he will ask, I wait for him to break the silence. But he seems to know when he can push me and when he can't, and I don't understand how a man who was a complete stranger yesterday knows me this well.

Holding my stare, he reaches behind him and tugs his shirt over his head, and the anticipation of seeing him naked, of being naked with him, drums wildly through my body. But he puts his shirt over my head, the spicy scent of his cologne teasing my nostrils. "What are you doing?" I ask, reluctantly shoving my arms through the sleeves.

"Making sure you know I'm here to stay. I'll be here with you tonight. I'll be here with you in the morning. And you'll still be wearing my shirt then—because we both know you have no clothes in your suitcase."

SIX

I SHOVE AWAY FROM LIAM AND push to my feet. "I told you, my things are being delivered."

He's already towering over me, distractingly bare-chested, with a perfect sprinkle of dark hair over his pecs. "I'm not asking for answers," he assures me. "Explain it to me when you're ready."

But I will never be ready.

He removes his cell phone from his pocket. "I'm going to have the hotel deliver sheets and pillows."

"No. I didn't invite you to stay."

"You want me to."

"You can't stay."

"Do you *want* me to?"

Now it's a question, and yes. I want him to stay. I should say no, but the word won't leave my mouth. "It's not that simple."

He pulls me close. "Let me make it simple, Amy. You want me to stay. I want to stay. I'm staying." He strokes my hair. "And you need help. I'm going to help you, baby. You aren't alone."

A tornado of emotions rolls through me. Becoming his charity case is so far from being Cinderella, I'd rather be alone. "No," I hiss. "I don't want your help."

"You *need* my help."

Angry and mortified, I demand, "How did we go from you fucking me properly, to me being a needy girl you want to help?"

"Correction. You're the gorgeous woman I still plan to fuck properly, many times over if I have my way. And there's someone who needs help in my path every day, and I help where I can. But I'm here with you because you are you."

"Stop saying that," I blurt. "You don't even know who I am."

"But I want to."

And that's the problem. I also want him to, but he can't. "This was just going to be one night."

He looks amused. "I don't remember coming to that agreement, so I'd better start making my case for two. By making tonight good for you."

Does he think a world-shattering orgasm wasn't good enough?

He dials a number on his phone. "This is Liam Stone," he informs the person on the other end. "I checked into the presidential suite about thirty minutes ago. Right. Everything is fine, but I'm at a friend's apartment across the street and one of her moving boxes is missing. She needs queen-sized sheets, pillows, a blanket, towels, and toiletries. I'll pay double your listed price to have them brought across the street to me, and whoever delivers the items will be well rewarded."

I press my hand to my face and turn away from him, walking to the end of the hallway to stare at the apartment that isn't mine, but is all I have. What have I done by bringing Liam here? He's determined to help me now, and he has money to uncover whatever he wants to uncover. If my handler doesn't have my bases well covered, Liam will find out who I am. And that could get him and me killed.

"Perfect," I hear Liam say, his voice closer. "And just to

be clear, I have the suite indefinitely, if you could make sure that's on record."

Indefinitely? The idea that I could be across the street from this man and simply ignore him, as I'd briefly hoped, is obviously pure insanity. You don't just ignore Liam Stone if he doesn't want to be ignored.

I turn around to find him only a few steps away, and my gaze lands on his flat, naked stomach. My mouth goes instantly dry—and not just because of his lack of clothing, which would be enough in itself. The number 3.14 is tattooed over the mathematical symbol pi, which frames his belly button. Beneath the symbol, rows of numbers that represent pi's infinite value form an inverted triangle that trails downward to disappear alluringly into his pants.

"What options do we have for food at this hour?" Liam asks whoever he's talking to, and the sound of his voice snaps my gaze up. His playful tone is laced with male satisfaction. He leans on the edge of the wooden dining room table and holds the phone away from his mouth. "Is pizza okay, and if so, what kind?"

Pizza, Amy. Stop thinking about where those numbers stop. "Cheese. I like cheese." I head to the kitchen, needing space, needing to think.

Inside the tiny room, I look for something to do to stay busy, to focus myself. I open the cabinets to see if I have any supplies. Nothing. No food or dishes, nothing to organize or clean. No place but Liam to put my mind, and he's no longer an escape. He's just trouble.

Pressing my hands to the counter, I let my head fall between my shoulders. I have nothing but the clothes on my back—actually, now on the hallway floor—and there's a billionaire standing a few feet away. The contrast is hard to miss.

Liam's voice grows closer again, deep and confident; he's a man who owns his world, whereas I do not own mine. I think maybe *he* owns my world more than I do right now, and that's a sign that I need some time alone. I'm weak tonight, but I'll claw my way back to strength again tomorrow. I have no choice.

I hear him order two large pizzas, one cheese and one pepperoni, as well as a diet Sprite, and I'm far too pleased that he remembered that from the plane. The man has become impossibly, frighteningly involved in my world in just one day.

"Food and supplies should be here in about fifteen minutes."

I turn to find Liam standing in the kitchen archway, his dark hair rumpled, his broad, glorious chest bare. But the mix of tenderness and lust in his eyes is what steals my breath.

"You didn't have to do that," I whisper.

"We need to eat."

"That's not what I mean, though I appreciate the food. You didn't have to order the hotel to bring me things. That costs money, and—"

He advances on me and I start to back away, but he's already in front of me, his hands on my waist. I suck in a breath, and just that fast, I'm sitting on the counter, skirt up again, knees apart, one of his hands tunneling into my hair. His mouth slants over mine, his tongue licking into my mouth, and he tastes like the raw, honest passion he's promised. And he tastes like me. It's a sultry, arousing thought. I sink deeper into the kiss, and tangle my fingers into his dark hair.

He tears his mouth from mine. "I told you I don't do anything because I have to. And I don't. But being inside you right now, baby—that I *have* to do. I need to. Right here in the kitchen." He pulls his shirt over my head and I wrap my arms around him, pressing my naked breasts to his chest. He strokes a hand down my hair, brushing his lips over mine. "This isn't going to be proper, but I'll make it up to you. Put your hands on the counter behind you."

"What?"

"Do it, Amy. Let me look at you."

The reticence life has taught me freezes me, but Liam

isn't discouraged. He presses my hands to the counter with his. "Leave them there."

I'm so nervous and aroused, I don't speak.

He brushes his lips over mine. "Say 'yes,' Amy."

"Yes," I whisper, and he smiles.

"You are so damned sexy."

"I don't feel sexy right now."

"Then what do you feel?"

"Out of my league." It's a relief to actually say what I really feel.

"If anyone's out of their league, baby, it's me. You're an angel and I'm . . . not." He glances up at the ceiling, as if he's struggling with something, before his stormy gaze returns to mine. "Maybe that's the appeal for both of us. We're different, dark and light. Right and wrong. Now don't move, or I'll show you just how not an angel I am."

The threat is darkly erotic, arousing, but it doesn't stop me from seeing the pain and self-loathing deep beneath his surface that I relate to far too well. I want to know what made him, what drives him, and what haunts him in the night. And I want to be the angel he sees me as, though I left that version of me in the past.

I will never be an angel to anyone but him, and that will be for just one night. "I won't move my hands, Liam. Not if you don't want me to."

His eyes dilate, darken, his jaw tightening into a hard line—not the reaction I'd hoped for. His hands move from mine to rest on my shoulders. "Now I'm going to fuck you, Amy." There's a new gruffness to his tone and I almost feel as if he's trying to shock me. Then he drags his fingers downward, trailing over my breasts to caress my nipples. His touch is light, teasingly gentle, and when it's gone I gasp with the deep ache in my sex, where I want him to be. "I don't like the way you won't let me touch you."

"You can touch me." He unzips his pants and shoves them, along with his underwear, down, his hard cock jutting forward, thickly veined. Then he reaches in his pocket and pulls out his wallet. "Later."

I only have tonight. "Promise me," I insist, needing his agreement. "I need you to promise me, Liam." My voice is raspy, filled with emotion that reaches beyond touching him. I want more, and I don't even know what "more" is.

He sets his wallet on the counter, a wrapped condom now in his hand, and presses his palms to my knees. "I promise, Amy." He leans in and kisses me, his mouth lingering on mine as if he is savoring me, and I feel the connection to this man in some deep part of my soul. I can't explain it. Maybe I just need to create this in my mind to survive the day, or to justify what I'm doing. But it's right for me now. He's right for me now.

His gaze holds mine as he tears open the wrapper, and my heart thunders in my ears and my sex aches with the emptiness in me that only he can fill. He looks down to quickly roll the condom on, and in seconds his mouth is back on mine, each delicious swipe of his tongue seducing me more. He's a drug that delivers passion and escape.

He curves a hand under my backside and lifts me, his gaze raking over my breasts, heating my skin, and then his other hand slides his cock along the sensitive lips of my sex, back and forth, until I'm panting with anticipation.

"Please, Liam," I whisper, desperate to feel him inside me.

The instant I issue the plea, he presses inside me and drives deep, filling me, stretching me, both of his hands now cupping my backside, arching my hips just how he wants them. He sinks in, burying himself to the deepest part of my body, and pleasure slides over his features. "Oh yeah, baby. You feel like heaven." He lowers his head and licks one of my nipples, then suckles, and the sensation spirals straight to my lower belly. My sex clenches around him, and my hips arch.

"Liam," I pant, needing him to move.

His lips taste mine. "Say my name again."

"Liam," I whisper, and wonder why this appeals to him. What it means, or if it means anything at all.

"What do you want?" he asks, his voice gravelly, laden with desire for me.

"You know what I want."

"Tell me." He reaches between us and strokes my clit.

"You *know* what I want." My voice is louder now, laced with the urgency building inside me, and I wrap my legs around his hips, touching him the only way I can.

"Say it, Amy. It's just you and me. Raw and honest. Give it to me."

Honest. That freedom is everything to me. "Fuck me. I want you to fuck me."

Another look of pure male satisfaction rolls over his face, and he slides his hands around my back. "Hold on to my neck," he commands. The instant I comply, he lifts me, melding my body to his, and he starts to pump, pulling me down on top of him at the same time. Pleasure nearly overwhelms me as each thrust of his cock sends shock waves of pleasure through my body. I bury my head in his chest and cling to him, the sound of his heavy breathing another stroke of silk on my nerve endings. I can feel his urgency, his need, and I'm there with him, pushing into him, trying to meet him, take him, find that sweet spot that we both want. And it's there, it's there, and his sexy growl tells me it's there for him, too. He grinds me against him, and my sex clenches around his cock, and I'm shaking or he's shaking, or we both are. A haze of pleasure rushes through my body, and I'm clutching him and he me, his arms around my back.

"That's what you call fast," he murmurs against my neck, kissing it. Then he leans back to search my face. "What are you doing to me, woman? I'm never . . ." He scrubs his jaw, seeming almost rattled, before his hands go to the counter at my hips. "Next time will be slow, baby. Nice and slow."

Next time. I'm pleased with these words, and stunned that I affect him so powerfully. I surprise myself by smiling. "I didn't even get to examine the many attributes of pi."

His lips curve. "Baby, you can examine it, lick it, do whatever you want to do to it and me—after I feed you. I promised, and I meant it."

Lick it. Yes. Please. Promise. I am not used to promises. I'll take this one and put it to good use.

He pulls out of me and I gasp. "Warning, please."

He laughs, a gentle lion's laugh, deep and sensual. I love that laugh.

"We have to get you dressed before they show up with the food and linens. " He sets me on the floor, then eyes the condom. "I'll be right back." He heads out of the kitchen, probably to the bathroom, and I suddenly realize I don't even have basics like toilet paper. This is *truly* embarrassing. I'll have to find a twenty-four-hour store and get some basic stuff. That's all there is to it.

I wiggle my skirt down my hips and pick up his shirt,

but I don't put it on. Liam will need it to answer the door.

His words play in my mind. *Be inside you now. I have to.* I smile to myself at the idea of making a man like Liam "have" to do anything, as I hunt down my panties, bra, and blouse—which appears to be missing a middle button. Nothing like a gaping front to show off your bra. Heading to the living room, I can hear Liam talking to someone on the phone from the bedroom, telling them how to find the entrance to the building. Knowing we'll have company soon, I quickly shove my clothes into my carry-on bag and pull out the T-shirt I bought at the airport before leaving New York.

"The bellman is coming up in the elevator now," Liam says, rounding the doorway just as I pull the T-shirt into place. He stops dead in his tracks, his expression suddenly turning stormy and intense.

Feeling very awkward at his reaction, I hold up his shirt. "I thought you might need this, and I tore the button off of my blouse."

He stalks forward and stops directly in front of me. "I have never hated an 'I love New York' T-shirt more than the one you have on."

His voice is a tightly pulled cord. He's angry, and I'm baffled. "You hate 'I love New York' shirts?"

"I hate what it says about your situation."

A knock sounds on the door, but he doesn't move. Silent

seconds tick by between us and I think he must be able to hear the thundering of my heart. Another knock and he turns away, pulling his shirt over his head as he stomps toward the door.

I wet my dry lips, feeling like an ice pick is chipping away at my nerve endings. I hate what this shirt says about my life, too. And I hate that Liam knows what it says about my life. I hate it because it means tonight must be our only night—even though a part of me was slipping into a fantasyland where I could allow Liam to be my Prince Charming for just a little bit longer.

I'm back in reality now, though. And no matter what happens tonight, it leads to one thing and one thing only: Tomorrow, I'll be alone.

SEVEN

LIAM HAS DONE HIS BEST TO convert my apartment into his penthouse suite for me.

I wait by the kitchen table, where two pizzas fresh from the hotel kitchen wait for us, and listen as Liam sees two hotel staff members out the front door, no doubt tipping them well. In all of fifteen minutes since their arrival, I now have everything I would have had in his suite: bedding and pillows, enough paper products, plastic utensils, kitchen items, and basic toiletries to last me for days, a hair dryer, hotel slippers, and a robe. My kitchen is stocked with canned sodas and a coffeepot with supplies, including cups. I am regretting my decision to stay here rather than go to his room, and not just because he's spent a pretty penny on me. It's because I am surely the talk of the hotel now, and Liam is exposed by his connection to me.

Dragging a hand through his thick, dark hair, looking tired but incredibly sexy, Liam walks back into the room. "The pizza smells good."

"Yes," I agree, but my mind is elsewhere and I hold my hands out to indicate the whole apartment. "Liam, this is all too much."

"It isn't even close to too much."

"It has to have cost you a small fortune."

"I have a fortune, Amy." And he sounds almost . . . bitter? About being rich? He grabs the pizza boxes, a couple of sodas, and plasticware, and motions to the bedroom. "Let's go eat on the bed."

Dinner in bed with the sexiest man I've ever known? I don't have it in me to complain. "Yes, okay, but thank you for everything. Thank you so very much."

"It's not your thanks I want."

"Then what do you want?" And I don't know why, but I hold my breath, waiting for his answer.

He tilts his head and studies me a moment. "For you to share dinner in bed with me."

I let the air trickle from my lips. It is the perfect answer, even if I sense it wasn't what he really wanted to say. "I'd like that."

I excuse myself to go to the bathroom and quickly change into some shorts I purchased when I bought my T-shirt. While doing so, I begin to worry dinner is an opening for Liam to drill me with questions. But I don't let myself linger in the bathroom, where I'm dodging the mirror. I won't like what I see in it.

Reassuring myself that I'm good at dodging what I don't want known, I join Liam on the bed. With my legs curled to my side, and the pizza boxes on the mattress between us, I dig into a slice of pizza with a hunger for something no one can take from me. My love of cheese pizza is one of the personal parts of me that no name or location change can strip away.

"Why don't I tell you about your neighborhood?" Liam suggests, dusting off his hands, after digging into his food with a heartiness that's double mine.

"You know it well enough to tell me about it?"

"Yes. I consulted on a building project not far from here a few years back. I stayed across the street for a month. When you come out of the building, go right a block and then left, and there are two coffee shops and several restaurants. If you go left instead of right when you exit, there's a mall two blocks straight down. There's a Whole Foods to the right of the mall and another grocery store to the left. You have everything from doctors to hair salons all in a small radius. A lot like New York. Which is good, since the city as a whole is not. Most people have cars, and I assume you don't have one of those being delivered tomorrow."

My heart sinks, and I fight the urge to set down my half-eaten second slice, afraid I'll give away how rattled I am. Instead, I pause on a bite and say, "No. No car," before chomping down on more than my food. I now have one more thing I haven't thought about and will have to face tomorrow.

"You do have your personal belongings being delivered, right?"

I abandon eating, setting down my slice and reaching for my soda, effectively avoiding eye contact with Liam. "Yes. I'll have my things tomorrow." It's not a lie, I tell myself. Whatever I buy will be here.

He shuts the lid to his pizza box and I set down my drink and do the same with mine. I'm not hungry. That's the thing about lies, or almost-lies. They make everything else harder to swallow along with them. I wonder if that's why he's ignoring the second half of his pizza. He can't swallow it with my lies, either.

And now he's just staring at me. He's good at that, I've discovered, really darn good at fixing me in his bright blue stare and seeming to see right through to my soul. His silence is almost as dangerous as his questions. He's analytical, a smart, calculated thinker. I see it in his eyes, and his job and his success back up my assessment. I have to get him to stop trying to piece together my story.

I scoot to the headboard, pull my knees to my chest, and work for diversion. "You don't seem like a recluse."

"Subject of your belongings avoided," he comments. "Check. That's one of the 'when you're ready' topics." Blood rushes to my cheeks, and he continues, "I learned about privacy from Alex, who was my mentor. He lost his wife and child in a car accident a year before I met him."

"Oh, God. How old was the child?"

He moves the pizza boxes to the floor and then sits against the headboard beside me, and we turn to face each other. "I never saw a picture. Looking back, I think seeing her hurt too much."

I wish every day for a picture of those I've lost, and it terrifies me that I can no longer remember their faces. It terrifies me that Liam is so near, so able to read what I feel. It terrifies me that he won't be here tomorrow. "To lose a child must be the worst kind of pain."

His lips draw into a grim line. "I'm told it changed him. I didn't know him before it happened. He didn't talk about them, and he didn't do press or make public appearances.

When I began getting buzz for being an architectural prodigy, he told me the hype could go to my head and ruin me, and forbade *me* any press as well.

"I deviated from his no-press policy one time only, when Alex was still alive. It was a hard lesson I've never forgotten. My ego and desire to share my success with the world were satisfied at his expense. His personal story ended up in the papers. He went crazy on me and then crumbled. That day changed me forever. I forgot about my ego, and to this day I rarely grant interviews or do appearances."

A little part of me softens for Liam, and I don't know what comes over me. I reach up and touch his jaw. "Now I know why you're so tight-lipped about your accomplishments."

He takes my hand, and I'm somehow more complete because he's touching me. "I keep my private life private, and let my work speak for me elsewhere."

I want to tell him how much I envy the confidence and sense of identity that he doesn't need anyone else to validate. But if I do, he'll ask me about who I am and who I want to be. And even if I could talk freely, I couldn't tell him what I no longer know. "That still doesn't spell recluse to me."

"That started a couple of years ago, when a particular reporter hounded me about an interview. When I wouldn't give it, she wrote a scathing piece about me."

His thumb begins stroking my palm and heat is radiating up my arm, and seems to have set my vocal cords on fire. "Scathing?" I manage.

"It pretty much said, 'he's rich, talented, and good-looking, but the man is a recluse with the social skills of an ant.'"

I gape. "An ant? No, she didn't!"

"I assure you, *she did*."

My lips curve and I fight my laughter, and lose.

He leans in and brushes his lips over mine. "You think that's funny, huh?"

I curl my hand on his jaw and I'm charmed at how easily he shares his story, by how wonderful it is to talk to someone, to touch someone. To touch him. "That description is so over-the-top it's comical. And it's not you."

His hand slides to my hip. "Are you sure about that?"

I've spent my whole adult life reading people, sizing them up, weighing them by degree of potential threat, and I've trusted him from the moment I first found myself captured by his presence in the terminal. "Yes," I confirm, without hesitation. "I'm sure." The air shifts around us, crackling with electricity, and I'm empowered by how comfortable I feel with him, despite my situation and the disparity between my experience and his. "You *are* rich, talented, and good-looking, but I forgive you all of those things because you're charming and funny."

His eyes shadow, turbulence waving through the heat. "You were right earlier," he says, pulling me close, molding our bodies together, his hands spread wide on my back.

My hand lands on the hard wall of his chest and his heart thunders beneath my palm, telling me I've hit a nerve. "Right about what?"

"When you said that I let you see. But Amy—I see more than you want me to."

"Then stop trying."

"That's not going to happen." He brushes his lips over mine, his tongue licking into my mouth in a slow, seductive caress. "We've already gone too far to turn back."

My hand is on his cheek, my legs intimately entwined with his, neither of which actions I remember taking. "Yes," I whisper. "We've gone too far, Liam."

"And yet not far enough," he replies, stroking the hair from my eyes, his voice rough sandpaper and masculine heat.

The intensity of what I feel for this man hits me like an earthquake erupting from somewhere deep inside, a deep, dark crevice of my soul. My emotions are all over the place. I don't know where he is taking me, and I'm as desperate to find out as I am to stop him. The needs to run and hide, and stay and fight, are equally intense.

He must read this in me, because he softly orders, "Turn out the light, Amy."

Turn out the light. I do not question his command, acting on my need for self-preservation, I turn off the lamp on the nightstand, relieved at the sanctuary of the darkness. Liam's arms are even more of a sanctuary as he pulls my back against his chest, his hand splaying possessively across my stomach. My lashes lower and I relax into him. I don't know how he is both the refuge I run to and the reality I'm running from, but in this moment that is exactly what he is to me.

His hot breath fans my neck and his lips brush my ear, the delicate touch sending a shiver down my spine. I expect him to kiss me again. To touch me and to fuck me, as he's vowed. I want him. I *need* him tonight, and I inhale, savoring his now-familiar spicy scent. And this time, there is no memory splintering through my mind. There is just the darkness I hide inside, the soft bed, and the hard man holding me.

I BLINK INTO the light and don't move, trying to process where I am. An unfamiliar closet door is the first focal point I manage to identify. New apartment. Denver. Liam. I jerk to a sitting position, searching the room, but he's nowhere to be seen. My heart twists—he's gone. I glance at the digital bedside clock the hotel brought me last night. It's eleven o'clock; of course he's gone. I was one of his many flings, and he has work to do.

How have I slept this late? How did I sleep at *all* in my state of mind, and without any nightmares?

I'll keep Godzilla at bay, Liam had said on the plane. And he had. Somehow, he gave me enough peace to get through the night. I'm pretty sure my mind used Liam as an escape, the way we used each other for sex. He gave me something outside my situation to focus on, which allowed me to shut down mentally and hold myself together. He'd been an unexpected gift. Who is now gone.

Standing up, I push down the empty feeling of being alone. I've done this for years, and I can do it again now. Besides, I was never fully alone, or my handler wouldn't have known when I was in trouble. His existence comforted me in the past, but it doesn't work this time. I can't go through this again. I have to have an exit strategy of my own. One that gets me off everyone's radar—including my handler's.

I walk to the living room to assess the rest of the apartment in the daylight and my breath hitches as I spot a package sitting on the kitchen table with a note. I reach for the wall to steady myself, an icy chill sliding through me at what this means. My handler has a key to the apartment.

EIGHT

THE AIR FEELS THICKER, MY BREATHING is more labored, and I barely remember walking to the table. I am simply there, staring down at what has been left for me. The box is white with an Apple logo on the top, and this does not seem like good news to me. Is the new phone I received last night, and haven't used, already compromised in some way? Am I moving again? Is this location unsafe? My adrenaline spikes and I grab the small white envelope and pull out the card.

Amy—

It's not safe to be without a phone. This is yours to keep and the service is paid for a full year. And don't say no, when I'm not there to argue the many reasons there are to say yes. Think about your safety and convenience. Besides, I selfishly don't want to wait to hear your voice until I see you again. My number is programmed in the phone. Text me when you get this and I'll call you during a break from my meeting.

Liam

A sense of relief washes through me and I become aware of my free hand balled at my chest, where my heart is beating like a drum. I inhale and will it to slow. I'm okay. Everything is okay. The note isn't from my handler. I am not leaving another city. I am not running. I am only hiding. Or maybe I am running. I don't know how to define what I am or what I do anymore, and suddenly I am exhausted when I've only just woken up.

I sit down and touch Liam's signature, blocking out everything else. He didn't walk out the door without saying good-bye. He doesn't intend to say good-bye at all. I'm blown away that he took the time to go buy me a phone before heading to his meeting. No one has done anything like this for me since I was still living at home.

Home. The past crashes over me. Sometimes I dream of returning there. Sometimes I think that facing the danger rather than running from it is a better option. But how do you face what you don't really know?

My gaze falls on Liam's neat, masculine script, and I briefly indulge in the memory of Liam's velvety, warm kisses and sensual caresses. I remember the pi tattoo and the numbers that formed a triangle that disappeared deliciously below his belt line. I remember his husky voice when he'd said, *"Baby, you can examine it, lick it, do whatever you want to do to it and me, after I feed you. I promised, and I meant it."*

A shiver of pure desire travels down my spine—but then my eyes land on the envelope with my lease inside, cutting through the sultry veil of fantasy. My handler left this here, so he might have a key. Had he had a key to my first place in New York? I shiver again, and this time it is not with desire. I am creeped out in a big way. I'm having my locks changed.

I stand up, setting the note from Liam back on the table. He's a distraction and a problem I cannot afford. No matter how much I want to see him again, I can't. I won't. Sleeping through the sound of a feather dropping isn't an option to me, let alone relaxing with a man I barely know to the extent I sleep through the opening and shutting of doors. Liam was good for one night, a bridge to the next day in the face of a crisis I'm on the other side of. I hope.

THIRTY MINUTES LATER, I've showered and am looking ridiculous in my T-shirt, skirt, and high heels, which I intend to replace quickly. Without styling product and a flat iron, my hair is a light-blond poufball; I look like I stuck my finger in an electrical socket. My mother would have called me a "hot mess," and I try to hear her voice in my head, but fail. Which is why I normally don't try. Failing hurts.

Giving up on my appearance, I pick up my small purse and head to the kitchen table to put all my new cards and ID in my wallet. Gathering up my lease and the cell phone I intend to return to Liam, I load them into the tote bag with my purse. I'll drop the phone by Liam's hotel sooner rather than later, to avoid running into him. Thanks to the to-do list I created, I feel more in control than when I woke up. Lists do that for me. I write things out when I need structure, and then I rewrite them if I still don't feel I have it all pulled together. Or I clean and organize. Or I write lists in between cleaning and organizing.

Maybe that should be my cover: I'll be a maid. No one would expect to find my father's daughter cleaning up after other people, and it would control my stress. It isn't nearly my dream career, or what I went to school for, but I have to find a way to get back to where I was before the museum, when surviving felt more important than dreaming.

I step into the hallway outside the apartment—I'm not ready to call it *my* apartment—and as I'm locking up, I hear the door directly behind me open and shut. I turn and find myself locked in the penetrating stare of a man as tall and devastatingly male as Liam, but that's where the comparison ends. While Liam has a worldly, refined, and edgy air about him, this man is a rugged bad boy from his torn, faded jeans to the long, light brown hair tied at the nape of his neck.

"New to the neighborhood?" he asks, shifting a leather backpack to one of his impressively broad shoulders. He's wearing a Dallas Cowboys T-shirt, and the link it represents to my home momentarily knocks my breath away.

"You okay?" he asks, and my gaze jerks to his. Was I that obviously rattled? I'm never obviously rattled. "You look like you saw a ghost."

"Yes, I'm new to the neighborhood," I say quickly. This could be a trap, a way to lure me into admitting some connection to a past I cannot claim. "I just moved in last night."

His gaze flickers over my clothing and lingers on my T-shirt. "Just a hunch," he comments, "but are you moving here from New York?"

"Yes," I confirm, embarrassed by the reminder that I'm a frizzy, mismatched mess, "and unfortunately my clothes didn't make it from the airport. This outfit certainly makes an impression." I sound nervous. I *am* nervous, about his intentions.

"I've lost a few bags in my time," he says, and his words are as warm as the interest I see in his eyes. He's oddly familiar, in a way I can't identify, but it doesn't make me uneasy. In fact, it's comfortable. "And," he adds, his voice a little softer, "I don't think you need a touristy T-shirt to make an impression." He motions to the elevators. "I'll ride down with you." He starts walking.

I stare after him. I don't need a T-shirt to make an impression? Is that good or bad? It's bad, I decide—I don't want to be leaving impressions of any sort on anyone.

I hurry to catch up, reminding myself that I have to fade into the background, play the mousy librarian like I have in the past. Though I've lost the library as a cover now. Anything I once did, I can no longer do.

We reach the elevator and he punches the button. "I'm Jared Ryan."

"Amy," I provide, and force myself to embrace this new

identity. "Amy Bensen. Nice to meet you. You live in the apartment across from me?"

"For a month or so," he says, but doesn't offer more. "What brings you to Denver?"

"A job." The doors to the elevator open and I step inside, changing the subject. "I hear there's a mall right up the street. That should tide me over until my bag arrives."

He steps into the car and presses the button for the ground floor.

Before he can ask any questions, I ask, "How far away is it?"

"Go left outside, cross at the stoplight and you'll be there."

I don't like how keenly he's looking at me, and his one-month stay is probably a good thing. The doors slide open and I don't waste any time escaping to the walkway outside, a high wind lifting my hair around my shoulders.

Jared joins me and motions down the sidewalk. "Just walk straight and you'll run right into the mall."

"Thanks. Nice to meet you."

He steps a bit closer. Really close, actually, enough so I can smell his cologne. It reminds me of Texas cedar on a spring day. He glances downward, his gaze landing on my feet, and he inspects my open-toed heels for so long, blood rushes to my cheeks. Over my feet. That's a new one.

His attention comes back to my face, his eyes narrowing. "Are you walking in those shoes?"

"Only until I can replace them at the mall," I try to say lightly.

"You want a ride?"

Yes. *No.* Not only does he see too much, he has an easiness that would make running my mouth far too easy. "Thanks, but it's close. And I'd like to explore my new neighborhood."

He considers my reply for a moment. "I'd offer to show you around, but I have a meeting."

It could be a polite, meaningless comment, but something in his eyes tells me it's not. And I would gobble up the opportunity to talk about my old home state—or really, to just talk about *anything.* If things were different. If I were really Amy Bensen.

"We're neighbors." My emotions make me sound hoarse, instead of casual and friendly, dang it. "I'm sure we'll see each other."

"I'm sure we will," he agrees, and there's a rasp to his voice that carries a hidden meaning. I search his eyes and I think . . . I think he feels this familiar, comfortable thing I feel, too.

I lift my hand in farewell. "See you soon." I turn and start walking, but my steps are heavy and slow, my body like lead, weariness seeping into my bones. I can feel Jared's stare, and I can feel him willing me to turn back around. And I want to. I want to with a desperateness I can barely contain. Working at the museum gave me a taste of what "normal" feels like, what friendship feels like, and I already miss Chloe badly. And I miss the tiny window of time when I walked around corners without fearing what was on the other side.

I pass two stores, and I swear I can still feel Jared watching me. But why would he? The hair on the nape of my neck prickles, and I start to think about Jared's Texas shirt and the way he questioned me about not knowing the area. And he feels familiar, but *why*? I'm suddenly glad I didn't ask about the shirt, and that I didn't answer his questions in any detail.

At the corner I stop by a bank and turn to face the door, pausing to look for Jared, but he's nowhere in sight. An odd sensation tightens in my belly and it's not comfortable at all. It's downright uncomfortable, which is crazy. I have every reason to be relieved that he is gone, and as I enter the bank and head for the cash machine to my left, I focus on what's knowable. Like how much money I have to survive on.

I pull my wallet from my purse and take out the ATM card I'd used in New York, staring down at it. The desire to claim my cash is powerful— but out of the blue, an image of Liam comes to my mind. He's a billionaire, a man who has the money to find out anything he wants to know about just about anyone, including me. How do I know that who-ever is chasing me doesn't have just as much money? What if my cards are flagged or tracked in some way?

I sigh with painful resignation and slip my card back into my wallet. If I touch that money it has to be on my way out of town, or maybe the country. But I'll keep the cash card and the old ID that lets me withdraw larger amounts, just in case.

Removing the new card my handler has given me, I slide it into the machine and punch in the code I've been given. My name comes up on the account, and I wonder how my handler set it up without my signature. My balance is $5000. My new rent is $2200, but it's already paid for this month. I'm too cautious to assume I really will get more money as promised, which means I need to hold on to two months' rent to feel secure. That leaves me with $600 for clothes and food.

My handler said he'd deposit weekly installments into this account, but starting when? Do I have utility bills to consider? I remove the card and head into the lobby. There's no way I'm letting anyone, even my handler, track me by my ATM card. I'm withdrawing all the money now.

FIFTEEN MINUTES LATER I'm in a dressing room in a store by the mall, wearing black shorts and a pink tank top, with cheap but cute black gladiator sandals on my feet. And what a relief they are. Between last night's escape and today, my feet are blistered—or, as my father used to say, my dogs are barking.

Deciding to wear my new clothes out of the store, I gather their tags and the other clothes I'm buying, ready to go to the cash register. Then the phone from Liam starts ringing. I sit down on the wooden bench in the dressing room, fighting the urge to answer it. I should have taken it to the hotel first, but the idea of walking into that fancy place in my T-shirt and skirt was too much.

Without making a conscious decision, I reach into my tote and pull out the box holding the phone. It stops ringing and then starts again almost instantly. I set the box down on the bench and stare at it, my stomach twisting. I'm a tangled mess. It stops ringing again, then there's a beeping sound. Liam has left a message, and I don't even think—as if to prove I am indeed a mess, I snatch up the box and open it, then listen to the message.

"I haven't heard from you, and we both know you're in

some kind of trouble. Call me, Amy. Don't text. I need to know you're okay. If I don't hear from you in the next fifteen minutes, I'm leaving my meeting and going to your apartment."

A thunderstorm of emotions rushes through me, and I let the phone drop to my lap. Liam is worried about me? He's going to leave a meeting to check on me? He barely knows me. Why would he do that?

We both know you're in some kind of trouble. I squeeze my eyes shut, conflicted clear to my soul. No one worries about me. No one should know enough to worry about me. But Liam does. He does, and I want him to. I want *him*.

The phone starts to ring again, and I can barely catch my breath. I have to talk to him, and I tell myself it's not because some deep part of me craves the sound of his voice. I have to turn him away and be convincing. For his safety. Money can buy things, and even people, but it can't keep him alive. It can't protect him from a threat I don't understand enough to explain.

I draw a breath and answer the call. "Hello."

"Amy," Liam says, and somehow my name is both a command and a caress.

"Liam," I reply, and I like how my name sounds on his lips. I also like how his name feels on my tongue. Even more,

I like how his tongue feels against mine, how he feels when I'm with him.

"You didn't text me like I told you to."

Normally I'd bristle at the command, but it takes too much effort. "I'm not good at taking orders, Liam."

"Is that why you didn't text me?" His voice is softer now, his tone too intimate and yet not intimate enough to satisfy the craving his voice creates in me.

I will myself to say good-bye, but I can't get the words out. I settle on, "I'm going to drop the phone by your hotel. I can't accept it."

"It's a gift."

"I pay my own way."

"The money is nothing to me, and everything to you."

This time I *do* bristle. Money is nothing to me beyond basic survival. "*Your* money is nothing to me, Liam."

"And while that would make me immensely happy any other time, Amy, it doesn't now. Money *is* just money, but your safety is another story. You need the phone."

I think of the phone my handler gave me, and it bothers me that he can track me. Maybe even see my phone records. Won't Liam be able to do the same? "I'll get my own phone."

"Use this one until you do."

I open my mouth to object, but he seems to read my thoughts. "A compromise, Amy."

Compromise. While I feel that's all I've done in my entire life, it's strangely appealing with Liam—maybe because it implies there's a relationship between us. But there can't be. "I can't keep the phone."

"At least use it until we can talk about it tonight."

"No. There isn't a tonight. I can't see you anymore."

Silence. One beat. Two. "There's that word again," he observes, then repeats, "We'll talk tonight, Amy."

"No, Liam. *No*."

"You think you're alone, but you aren't."

"Because I have you now?"

"Yes. I know you don't believe that, but you will. Soon, baby, you will."

The idea of having him is bittersweet in so many ways, I couldn't list them in a year. "You don't know what I think, or what's important to me."

"I know enough. The rest, I want to find out."

"No." But it sounds like *yes*. "I won't be here tonight. I have plans." Like locking myself in that cage of an apartment and going nowhere.

"I'm not going away, Amy. You do know that, don't you?"

His voice is possessive, a rasp of sandpaper over my nerve endings followed by pure silk, and it does funny things to my stomach. "I don't need a protector, Liam."

"I see things differently."

My spine locks into a steel bar. "I'm not your—"

"Not yet. But I want you to be."

I blink. *What* does he want me to be?

"I'll call you when I finally get out of this meeting. It will probably be about six. One of the investors isn't flying in until later today."

I fight the urge to ask about the meeting and the investor. "Why are you doing this?" I whisper.

"You won't like my answer."

"How do you know what I like or don't like?"

"I'll see you tonight." The line goes dead and I don't know why, but I need to hear his answer. I call back.

He answers immediately. "At least I have you using the phone."

"Why are you doing this?"

"Because you're you, Amy. And I have to go, but text me if you need me." He hangs up again.

I clutch the phone. He was right: I don't like his answer. My very existence is a lie—which means anything he sees in me, anything he sees between us, is also a lie.

NINE

AFTER BUYING THE CLOTHES, I HEAD for the Realtor's office. The six-block walk takes me past rows of cute stores and eateries, and I find Evernight Legal Services nestled between a coffee shop and a furniture store. I frown. I thought this was a real estate office, but it's logical that a law office might handle all kinds of business affairs for someone.

I head inside, nearly pushed through the door by a gust of wind that jangles the bells at the entrance. In New York, I was pushed and shoved by people. Here it's Mother Nature, and according to the store clerk I'd asked, this is normal.

Swiping at the hair in my face, I find myself in a small, homey-looking office, with a rich mahogany desk in front of a narrow hallway.

"Welcome." A gorgeous young blond bombshell wearing a hot-pink dress and lipstick to match appears behind the desk. "Can I help you?"

"Amy Bensen." The name rolls off my tongue far more easily than it did with Jared. I settle my leather bag, packed with my shopping haul, on the waiting room chair. "I'm here to drop off my signed lease."

"Oh, yes. Amy." She smiles and offers me her hand. "Luke told me you were coming by."

"Luke?"

"My boss. He's not in right now. I think he said there was a package for you."

A package? I'm not sure what to make of that. "For me? Are you sure?"

"Well, I'm new, so I could be wrong, but let me go look in the mail room. I'm almost certain we had something, though." She heads down the hallway.

The package has to be from my handler. *Maybe it contains a full explanation of what's happening and why I had to leave New York*, I think hopefully. My heart begins to pound in my chest. Answers. That's all I want. It's the unknown that makes me jumpy and afraid of my own shadow.

The woman returns with a box wrapped in brown paper, reading a sticky note that's attached. "Yep. The note says it's from Mr Williams."

Could he be my handler? "Have you met him?"

Her brow furrows. "Dermit Williams?" I nod and she shakes her head. "No. He's out of the country. He's been Luke's client for years, I believe."

I pull the lease from my bag. "Here's the signed paperwork I was told to bring by. I'm assuming Mr. Williams owns my building? The lease is with Evernight."

She shrugs. "I don't know, but that sounds logical. I really just started a few days ago." She offers me her hand. "I'm Meagan, by the way. You can call me Meg."

"Nice to meet you, Meg." I shake her hand. "Are you new to town, or just to this job?"

"New to town, just like you. I got my paralegal degree in New Mexico just this month, and had a job lined up with a big firm that fell through." She holds out her hands. "So here I am."

"Oh, no. I'm sorry. Why don't you go home?"

"Ex-boyfriend." She crinkles her nose. "You know. Personal drama, new life, yada yada. Life's as perfect as a hot man in a pink hat, if you know what I mean."

I try to picture Liam in a pink hat, and grin. It's so wrong. "I'm not going to forget that expression anytime soon."

She grins. "I aim to make a lasting impression."

I like Meg. I liked Jared. As for Liam, I downright crave him. None of this is good. None of this is staying off the radar.

"Since we're both new and all, we should do coffee, or drinks," Meg suggests, her voice bringing me back to the present. "There are some cool spots around here for happy hour."

"Sounds fun." And it does, but I won't be going, any more than I'll be calling to check on Chloe. I'm not that selfish, and I won't let a window of weakness change that.

"You want to exchange numbers?"

"I have a new cell phone, but it isn't working right. I'll call you and give you my number when I'm sure I'm keeping it." I crinkle my nose. "And when I remember the number."

"I did that last week. Let me give you my cell number so you don't have to call me here." She scribbles it down and hands it over.

Accepting the paper, I ignore the pinch in my chest at the certainty I will never be calling her. "Thanks. It's nice to start to know people here."

She lifts the box. "It's kind of heavy."

I take it from her and frown. It's going to be a long walk back to the apartment.

THE INSTANT I step out into the wind, I have the sensation of being watched. Two blocks later I still feel it, and it's driving me nuts. It's understandable paranoia, considering everything, but I don't remind myself again how I got past this in New York. I didn't get past anything. I put it out of sight, and out of sight was out of mind. Not this time. This time I want answers. And I hope this box holds them.

Finally, I reach the apartment and, with aching arms from lugging all my stuff, I walk inside, drop my bag, and lock the door. Holding the box to my chest, I lean against the door, listening for anything or anyone that might be present. Eerie silence greets me, and while it should comfort me, it doesn't. I hate silence. I hate it with a passion. I rush forward and set the box on the table, and with my heart in my throat, I search the apartment.

Once I'm certain I'm alone, I sit at the dining-room table, and in the absence of a kitchen knife, I struggle with the tape, using my apartment key to cut it down the center. Note to self: I need a key ring for the single key I'm bound to lose otherwise, and silverware. I start a kitchen shopping list in my mind. A couple of cheap pans. Paper plates. Plasticware, and a few real knives. I get the box open and set my key aside.

Lifting the lid, I stare down at the MacBook Air with a folder on top. This is certainly a surprise. I reach for the folder and flip it open. A typed note is included.

Ms. Bensen—

Welcome aboard. Enclosed is a list of the properties Evernight leases on my behalf. As we discussed in our phone interview, you will need to do a weekly visual inspection to ensure they are properly maintained, and e-mail me a report.

Phone interview? This is clearly a cover story. I keep reading.

An external check is all I need, and all properties are within a few blocks of one another in Cherry Creek. In addition, Evernight will provide you with a report on all newly listed properties in the Denver area. You will cross-reference them with public listings and send me anything that fits the criteria I'm including.

Please e-mail me when you get this so I know you are properly settled. I will have various other projects for you to undertake once I get to my location. I have limited phone connectivity, so if you have any issues you will need to e-mail.

If there is an emergency you can call my
attorney, whose number I'm including.

Dermit Williams
Dermit Williams Holding Company

I scan the folder and find a printed e-mail from my new boss. There's no handwriting, no symbol to tell me I should trust this person. I'm baffled. I've been told this job is my cover story. A fake cover story. Or maybe it isn't. Maybe this is a real job, just like my lease is a real lease. But the instructions I received clearly stated that I was not to get a job.

Looking through the folder, I see property listings. Maybe my boss isn't real. Maybe he, like the job, is a cover that is meant to be convincing.

This is *not* a comforting thought. It tells me I have reason to go deep into hiding.

I remove the computer from the box and find it's not new, but close. It powers right up and I create a Gmail account for Amy Bensen and e-mail my new boss. A muffled beeping sound reminds me that the phone Liam gave me is still in my bag by the door, and I head that way. Removing the phone, I find a text message.

Don't eat dinner. I want to take you out.

I press the phone to my forehead and try to weigh my worries for Liam's safety as valid or not. I have no real reason to believe anyone but me is in danger, and Liam has the money and resources to protect himself. But he can't protect himself from something he doesn't know about. And I don't know him well enough to risk trusting him, no matter how much my gut says I can.

The phone beeps and I look at the screen. Amy?

He's going to call me if I don't answer. I type, I'm here. I'm doing some work my new boss gave me. Call me when you head this direction.

Your new boss?

I frown. Yes.

Interesting. I can't wait to hear all about him.

Avoidance mode kicks into gear. What time will you be here?

Around six or seven. Headed into a meeting and I'm not sure how long it will take.

I glance at the clock. It's three. How did it get to be three? See you soon, then.

Not soon enough.

The words could be nothing more than a flirty message, but it feels like more. *He* feels like more. The very "more" I have ached for, deep in my soul. Which is exactly why I have to walk away. I will trust him. I will pull him into my hell. And then one or both of us will crash and burn.

AFTER TWO FRUITLESS hours of searching the internet for clues about my new boss, I leave a message for Meg about changing the locks on my apartment.

I know that seeing Liam again might send the wrong message, but it's a risk I have to take to return the phone. I considered just dropping it off, but I know he'll just march to my door. If I'm ending this, I need to really end it. No—not *if*. I *am* ending it. I'll meet him at the hotel bar, nice and public, and then be on my way.

Feeling jittery, I decide to run to the store to grab a few staples, hoping it will exhaust my nerves. It doesn't work. While I felt better during my little excursion, I'm right back where I started the instant I step into my "fake" apartment. I decide I probably need food, though it may not sit well on my stomach. Still, it's not like I have to worry about ruining the dinner I'm not having with Liam.

Deciding on a can of soup, I pull out one of my new pots from a shopping bag, and then grimace. I have no can opener or bowls. Paper plates aren't going to cut it. My list has failed me, and I jump on the excuse to get out of this cage.

The instant I step off the elevator, I know this trip is different from the last. Unease prickles through me and the hair at my nape lifts. The sensation of being watched is back, and each step I take magnifies the feeling. I speed up more and more, until I'm all but running as I reach the grocery store. At the door I glance behind me, searching for the source of my discomfort, but finding no one obvious. If I could flippantly call this paranoia, I'd gladly do so. But I'm not hiding for no reason. I'm trapped in a world that's black and white. Run or be caught. Hide or die, like everyone I loved has died.

Inside the store, I feel relief. The sensation of being watched is gone. I'm safe in a public place. But I'm still deeply troubled by the idea of being watched, even by my handler. *He saved my life*, I remind myself. He is trustworthy. No one else can be trusted. But Liam. I play that idea over and over in my head and in every version of how and I think of all the good ways that might end. And the bad. I think of him being in danger. I think of me being in danger.

Quickly, I fill my basket with my staple bargain popcorn, a few bowls, and a cheap can opener. As I head to the checkout line, the phone Liam gave me rings.

Steeling myself for the impact of his voice, I answer. "Liam?"

"Damn, woman, I like how you say my name."

My cheeks heat with the gruffness of his tone that tells me that he means his words. The knowledge that I affect him reaches inside me and tightens my belly. I barely feel like I exist in this world, but this rich, famous, and impossibly delicious man makes me feel as if I do. I don't want to let him go. I don't want to lie to him.

"I'll be there in a couple of minutes to pick you up."

The announcement jerks me back into the moment. "I'm at the grocery store. I'll drop off my stuff and meet you at the hotel bar."

"I'll pick you up."

"No. I want to change my clothes anyway." It's my turn in line, and I put my items on the belt. "I have to check out. I'll see you soon."

"Amy—"

I hang up, then cringe. Did I really just hang up on him? Maybe I should call him back—but the less I say before *good-bye*, the better. I'm still telling myself that five minutes later, when I walk out of the store.

As I'm about to cross the grass to the stoplight, a fancy black sedan pulls up beside me and stops. My heart lurches as the front passenger window rolls down. Holding my breath, I lean down to see that Liam occupies the driver's seat, and the man is power and sex in a black suit and a royal-blue shirt that brightens his blue eyes.

He reaches across the seat and opens the door. "Hop in, baby."

My stomach flutters at the endearment that he might use on all women, but it doesn't matter. Right now, he's using it on me. Right now his eyes are on me, and even with his playful tone, they're as intense as he is . And Liam Stone is as intense as they come.

"Is this your car?" I ask, trying to decide what to do. Getting in the car is a ticket to being mindlessly lost in the temptation that is Liam.

"Rental." He arches a brow at my stillness. "If you're worried I'll bite, I promise to tell you first."

My eyes go wide and he laughs, a sexy, rough sound from deep in his chest. The chest I want to touch again.

I glower at him. "I won't." The smart reply earns me another of his sexy laughs, and he's successfully seduced me right here on the street.

Caving to the inevitable, I step in and settle my bags on the floor of the obviously expensive car. I steel myself for the impact of being in a small space with him where I both long to be, but see it for what it is. A mistake. Being near this man is not going to help me say good-bye.

The expensive leather seat hugs my bare legs, and

Liam's earthy scent tickles my nostrils, teasing me senseless. It's official: this was a mistake. A wonderful mistake.

I tug the door shut and am immediately pulled into his arms, one strong hand sliding into my hair. "Miss me?" he asks, his breath a hot tease on my lips.

My fingers curl on his jaw, the soft rasp of new whiskers teasing my fingertips. I remember that rasp on my skin, and everything fades but the moment and the man. No one has ever done that to me. "Did *you* miss *me*?"

"I'll let you decide." His mouth slants over mine, his tongue parting my lips, caressing against mine in one lush stroke. "Do I taste like I missed you?"

I'm melting like chocolate in the hot sun, and he's barely touched me. But I want him to. Oh yes, I want him to. "I'm still not convinced."

His lips curve before he answers me by licking wickedly into my mouth, teasing me with two deep strokes of his tongue that leave me darn near panting. "Any doubt I missed you now?"

My chest burns. Liam missed me. I have been missed. This is unfamiliar territory, and I like it. And I am *so* not ready to let go of this man. "If I say yes, you won't kiss me again, right?"

"I'll do a whole lot more than kiss you when I get you alone." His promise is both soft velvet and rough sandpaper, and the air around us thickens, the sexual tension transforming into something far deeper than simple lust. Far harder to walk away from.

He strokes a tender hand down my hair and I lean into the touch like a cat claiming her territory, though he is not mine. He will never be mine.

"Hungry?" he asks.

"Is that a trick question?"

His lips curve. "I'll take that as a yes." He brushes his lips over mine. "Me too, baby. Me too." He releases me and leans back in his seat, and I'm instantly cold, though I was hot seconds before. He puts the car in drive and gives me a steamy look. "Buckle up and we'll be at your place in no time."

I don't argue, eager for anything that makes me feel grounded, certain he will take me on a proverbial wild ride before this night is over if I let him. And I can't let him. I squeeze my eyes shut, telling myself I won't do anything but accept the lift to my apartment. I'll make small talk and ease the sexual tension, and get back where I need to be, to do what I have to do.

"There's a great Italian restaurant next to the hotel, if you like Italian."

"I'm a pasta addict." My lashes lift as I reply, and I notice the logo on the dash. "You rented a Bentley?"

He shrugs. "They didn't have anything else."

I don't hide my disbelief. I've never even seen one, because they run in the six-figure range and I don't know people who pay that kind of money for a car. I don't even know many people who can afford to *garage* a car in New York, let alone pay for one like this.

"And," he continues, "it's the only car I thought was good enough to drive you around in."

"Me?" I purse my lips. "You, Liam Stone, are rich and spoiled. I am not."

"I'll spoil you if you let me." His voice is a soft, silky promise.

My chest burns with something I don't want to feel. "No." It comes out almost a hiss. "I don't want your money." *I just want a life.*

If he notices my tone, he doesn't show it. "Spoken like someone who has never had money."

Avoidance is always my friend. His questions are not. "Very few people have your kind of money."

"Which proves my point," he assures me.

"Which is what?"

"I have the money to spoil you, and I plan to." Then he shifts the subject as if he's stamped the topic done, approved, fact: "Do you have any groceries that will go bad, or can we go straight to the restaurant?"

I don't want food. I want to lick that tattoo of his before I say good-bye to him. That would keep him from asking questions. Until it's over, I remind myself. "I need to drop by my place and change."

His hot gaze flickers down my bare legs, and up again. "I like you like this."

My cheeks heat and my sex clenches. "You're in a suit."

"I'll change. You stay the way you are."

I open my mouth, but snap it shut before I tell him I like him just as he is. That isn't going to help my good-bye campaign—but then, neither did kissing him. "Either way, I want to freshen up."

Liam pulls the car up in front of his hotel and a doorman instantly helps me out of the car. By the time I'm standing, Liam is in front of me, reaching for my bags before I can stop him.

"I've got them," I say, reaching out to take them, and our hands collide, sending a tingling sensation up my arm.

My eyes dart to his, and I see the awareness in them. He, too, has felt the connection. Maybe this is only sex to him, or some need to protect me I can't understand, but it's real. It exists, and it's powerful.

"I'll meet you at the hotel bar in thirty minutes," I choke out from my suddenly dry throat.

"You said you didn't want to go to the hotel with me."

"Not to your room. Hotel bars are open to the public."

His eyes narrow, suspicion etched in their depths. "I'll help you with your bags."

"They're very light. I'll meet you in twenty minutes."

"I'll walk you to your door."

"If you come to my apartment, we'll get distracted." For once, I get to speak the truth.

He arches a brow. "Is that supposed to discourage me?"

"Yes," I reply tartly, and the urge to kiss him one more time before I deliver the good-bye is too intense to fight. I push myself to tiptoe and lean in to him, hands flattening on the hard wall of his chest, and press my lips to his. He's stiff, unyielding, and I'm instantly uncomfortable, second-guessing my boldness. I begin to pull back when he drops my bags to the ground and pulls me close, his hand sliding up my back, his tongue licking into my mouth in one long, hot sweep that has me moaning into his mouth.

When his lips leave mine I'm shocked at the scene we've made, too embarrassed to look around and find out who's watching.

"I just want to make sure you know how much I want you, no matter what. And you're right. If I come with you to your apartment, we won't leave anytime soon."

He sets me away from him, and to my horror grabs my bags from the ground and looks inside. His gaze lifts, brow arching. "Plasticware?"

The warmth his declaration about wanting me had created turns cold. "I haven't had time to unpack."

"So your things were delivered today?"

"My things are just fine."

I reach for the bags and he shackles my wrist. "Amy—"

A horn honks, saving me whatever command is certain to come out of his too-tempting mouth. "We're making a scene. I'll see you in a few minutes."

His jaw flexes, tension in his face. "I'll be waiting." He releases my bags, and I waste no time in leaving. I am so tired of running away.

TEN

TWENTY MINUTES LATER I'VE CHANGED INTO a simple, versatile little black lace dress I scored for twenty-nine dollars on a bargain rack. With my heels it's a bit sexy, but I'm dressing up to feel confident, not to impress Liam. I'm so good at lying, I almost convince myself that's the truth.

I check my reflection in the mirror and argue with myself about ending things with Liam. I begin with all the reasons I don't have to say good-bye. I've dated other men. I had a dormmate, and although we didn't bond, we lived together. Liam can handle himself far better than anyone I have ever known. But he's also the only person I've ever known with the resources to dig into my past and get himself killed in the process. I won't let that happen.

Resolve in place, I head for the elevator and ride to the bottom level. The doors ding open and I'm surprised to find Jared standing there. He grins at the sight of me, all sexy male charm and hotness. "Ditched the T-shirt, did you?"

"I did," I agree, finding myself smiling despite my nerves over Liam. I step out of the car and expect Jared to move aside to catch the door. He doesn't, and we're toe-to-toe. The sense of familiarity with this man is instant, and I freeze, unable to move away. I am terrified of this piercing black hole that I know too well will suck me into a place where everything and everyone is a potential threat. I swore I would never return to this place, but I feel the fingers of the beast reaching for me, pulling me inside.

"You're supposed to take that out of the box."

I blink Jared back into focus. "Box?"

He glances down and I follow his gaze to the iPhone box I wasn't able to fit into my small purse. "Oh." I lift it slightly. "I like the box. I'm a rebel that way."

He laughs. "A woman out to seduce me."

I snort, a ridiculous sound that makes my answer all the more meaningful. "I'm the last person to seduce anyone."

His light brown eyes fill with the amusement I intended to spark. "You had me at the T-shirt and high heels," he teases.

"You're never going to let me forget that, are you?"

"Probably not." He flicks a quick look up and down my body. "Does the dress mean your things arrived okay?"

This is almost the same question Liam asked me earlier and my mood instantly swings from comfortable to uneasy. I make a weak attempt at a smile. "All is well in Amy Land." I've barely spoken the lie when the cell phone begins to ring inside its box. Jared arches a brow and I quickly say, "Late to a dinner thing. I should run."

"So you have friends here already?"

Avoiding a lie I might have to remember later, I shrug. "Guess the T-shirt and heels were an ice-breaker. Good-night, Jared."

"Goodnight, Amy."

There's a softer quality to his voice that I feel I've heard before. Something about his tone strikes a memory, and a chill slides down my spine. Spots begin to form in front of my eyes, and—oh no. No. No. Let it stop now. *Please* let this not be happening.

But it's too late. The pinching sensation in my forehead that I haven't felt in years begins to form. I sway, and Jared grabs my arm. Reflexively, my hand goes to his chest.

"Whoa," he murmurs. "What just happened?"

I can't open my eyes. I don't even try. "Blood sugar," I whisper; the excuse I always used when these spells hit me. "I'm fine."

"You don't seem fine." He sounds worried.

Worried is not good. Worried will get me an ambulance, and attention I don't need.

I inhale and the air feels like lead in my lungs, but the pain is good. It wakes me up and brings me back. "I am." I force my eyes open and the spots begin to fade. Relief washes over me. "Really," I assure him." I already feel better." Except that my hand is on his chest. Appalled, I jerk it back.

He chuckles. "Easy. You'll tumble over."

"No. I'm steady now."

He releases my arm. "That kind of reaction will kill a man's confidence, you know."

I seriously doubt this man has confidence issues. "Sorry. I was just embarrassed."

"Don't be embarrassed." His voice is a gentle caress.

More of that familiarity creeps into my mind, and the spot on my forehead starts to tingle just as my phone rings again. The sound is music to my ears, a welcome escape from another episode, and from Jared.

Jared's lips quirk. "You really need to ditch the box."

"Or get a bigger purse," I say, sounding like a complete

idiot. I'm officially ready to get the heck out of here. "Thanks for the save. I'll see you around."

For the second time today I take off running, only this time I'm running *to* Liam, not away from him. And that feels so much more right than the good-bye I have to deliver.

I approach the hotel in a gust of wind that has my dress lifting. I struggle to capture the skirt and manage to shove the material down, and through the wild mass that once, thanks to my new flat iron, *was* my sleekly groomed hair, I watch the doorman smirk and nod. Blushing, I hurry past him, wondering if he also saw Liam and me tongue-dancing in front of the hotel earlier.

This night is off to a grand start. I was right when I decided to change clothes; I need all the confidence I can get to survive the next fifteen minutes.

Stopping inside the doorway, I spot the sign for the restaurant and bar directly ahead. Even here, a good twenty feet away, I can already hear the rumble of voices over the sound of music coming from inside the arched entryway. Though I don't know Liam well, my instincts say he won't like my choice of location.

As if he's heard me, Liam exits the bar, irritation etched on his handsome face, and his eyes collide with mine.

His expression softens and warms, and I watch his frustration melt away, as if seeing me makes everything all right.

I don't move to meet him, frozen in the bittersweet knowledge that seeing me has pleased him. He walks toward me, his jacket gone, his lean masculinity accentuated by the dark dress pants and fitted blue shirt; he is power and grace, the epitome of dark good looks.

The instant he stands before me I'm captivated by his deep blue stare, lost in a sea of warm, drugging water. I want to swim a little longer, but too quickly, his gaze lowers to the box I'm holding, and my gut twists with the knowledge that my time is up.

I hold it out to him. "I can't take this." While I am proud of how strong my voice sounds, my hand shakes, practically drawing a storyboard of my emotions that Liam is too smart to miss. Anger fills me at how the past has made me weak. I should never have taken the job at the museum and let it back into my life. But then I would never have met Liam, and I'm not sure I can wish him away, even if I have to walk away.

"Let's talk about it over dinner."

I shake my head, more at my desire to agree than at his words. "I can't go to dinner. I can't see you anymore." I sound like I mean it. Almost.

Those piercing blue eyes sharpen, and the dark edginess he wears like a second skin ramps up about a hundred notches. Seconds tick by, and I try to think of some appropriate thing to say, when I, of all people, know less is better.

Should I turn and leave? Yes. but I'm still holding the phone. He needs to take it.

He takes the phone, but he doesn't stop there. He interlaces the fingers of his free hand with mine. "Come with me."

My eyes go wide, but he's already tugging me along with him—and not toward his hotel room. I don't have time to consider why that disappoints me. Not when he's headed toward the exit, which most likely means he intends to go to my apartment, where he'll discover the delivery of my things has not taken place.

Desperation kicks in and I rush forward, putting myself in front of him, flattening the hand he isn't holding on his chest and digging in my heels. "Take me to your room." I can't believe I've just said that, but the warm spot in my belly won't let me take it back.

Liam's jaw flexes. "You can't see me anymore, but you want me to take you to my room?"

His voice is tight, a band of steel wrapping each word. He's angry. I don't know why, though the possibilities are many. I'll figure it out when we are effectively detoured from my apartment, which would surely lead him to dig where it is dangerous to dig. "Yes. I want to go to your room. I need to, ah . . . lick your tattoo good-bye."

"I'll keep that in mind."

My cheeks heat at the edge in his voice, but I will myself past my discomfort. "Liam—"

He takes a small step and I dig in my heels and wrap my fingers around his shirt, wrinkling the fine material. Direct is all I have left. "I don't want to go to my apartment."

"We aren't." This time he firmly sets me aside, and before I can so much as yelp, he has my hand in his, and we're headed for the exit.

I follow, trying not to look around me and spot attentive observers of our exchange. For a supposed recluse and a woman on the run, I'm pretty sure we've made our second scene of the day, and I'm not looking for a third. We pass the sliding glass doors and I avoid the gaze of the doorman.

Liam turns away from my apartment to the right, where people stroll here and there, and thankfully the wind is milder, and my skirt stays at my knees.

I cast him a sideways look. "Where are we going?"

He stops abruptly and faces me. "The phone's in your name. You have to talk to them about the service."

"Oh." Disappointment hits me hard and fast. I've become complicated. He's ready to cut all ties with me. His "not going anywhere" vow sure didn't last. But . . . he's holding my hand. Why would he hold my hand if he was cutting all ties? It's not like he'd worry about losing the phone; he's a freaking billionaire.

"Oh?" he prods.

"Oh," I repeat to keep myself from saying something like, "Can we go back to the hotel and start this night over?" I need to stick to my plan. Saying good-bye is the right thing to do. "I'm not phone-savvy," I finally manage. "If you need me to go with you, I will." My gaze flickers to our connected hands, and the quick pinch in my chest that provokes has me jerking my eyes back to Liam's. "Where is it?"

"Two blocks." His gaze drops to my feet, where it lingers and then rakes hotly up my body. Jared's inspection this morning had been a bit too familiar; Liam's is downright wicked. And oh my, I'm hot all over and tingling in places I shouldn't be tingling in public. He knows, too. I see it in the quirk of his lips, the gleam in his eyes as he asks, "Can you walk that far in those shoes?"

"After walking around New York for years, my feet are oblivious to pain. I can walk." Or I might stand here in the beam of his scorching gaze and melt in my shoes. He still wants me, but it will be cold comfort in my empty bed tonight. I'm letting him go. He's letting me go. I'm complicated. I'm always complicated.

I start to turn, to get this over with, but his fingers curl on my elbow and he pulls me close, his legs pressing to mine, sending waves of heat through me. And just like that, everything but Liam fades away. There are no people walking about; there's no doorman a few steps away, no horns honking. There is just me and this man, and I tingle with awareness, finally alive when I was barely living before I met him. There are so many things I want to say to him but can't. I'm confused and conflicted in all ways possible with this man, stuck between right and wrong.

"Liam—"

"Amy," he says softly, his tone just sharp enough to be a warning. Maybe he simply wants me to stop arguing with him, but he's also saving me from something I might say and we'll both regret.

"Yes," I say, wishing he'd say whatever he stopped me to say. Wishing it would be something magical that made everything all right. "Let's go to the phone store, Liam."

I don't know why I said his name. Why I felt the absolute need to say it, or why it lingered on my lips almost wistfully. But his eyes narrow, his head tilting slightly, and there's no question he noticed. I hold my breath, not sure what he'll say. Not sure what I want him to say.

But when he finally replies, I get only, "Yes. Let's go to the store."

I'm both relieved and disappointed by his non-response. But he doesn't allow any distance between us, drawing my hand into his again as he turns us forward. Easily, comfortably, we fall into step together, silence settling between us. I find myself obsessing about our fingers twined together, about what that means about his intentions, and even mine.

Too quickly we are at the store, and Liam releases my hand to open the door. I freeze with a sudden jolt of reality. We are not one but two now, and he may never touch me again. Once we're done here, we are *done*.

Emotion wells in my chest and I can feel Liam looking at me, willing me to look at him, but I can't. Not without forgetting why I have to do this.

Feet heavy as lead, I walk into the store, the air-conditioning adding to my chill. Hugging myself, I stop just inside the entrance and gaze at the phone displays in the center of the store, the accessories hanging on the walls, and the small service counter in the back. Liam steps up beside me, and as if to wash away my fear that he'll never touch me again, his hand settles on my back. The touch is electric, sizzling down my spine and burning away the cold.

"Hi, folks." The greeting comes from a lanky guy of no more than twenty, with dark, wavy hair and black, thick-rimmed glasses, wearing a store T-shirt. "I'm Scott. Can I help you?"

"We need to have you look up our account information," Liam states.

Scott shoves his glasses up his nose and indicates the counter in the back of the store. As we follow him there, Liam doesn't remove his hand from my back. We stop at the counter and Scott walks around behind it, pulling a keyboard closer to him. "What can I help you with?"

Liam sets the phone on the counter. "Can you confirm the name on the account, and who has access to it?"

Scott's face pinches. "Only if I'm talking to the person who owns the account, and surely they would know that information already."

"Not if a good friend set the account up for them," Liam corrects.

"Then I need the ID of whoever is on the account," Scott replies. He obviously takes his job seriously, and I respect the guy, considering how much I value my privacy.

Liam glances at me. "He'll need your ID."

I'd seen this coming, but as I open my purse a sliver of unease ripples down my spine as a thought hits me. Is this Liam's way of seeing my driver's license? I remove my Colorado driver's license. Liam is a smart man; this is going to make him ask questions.

I slide the license forward facedown and hold my breath, hoping that Scott is discreet.

He lifts it and sets it on a keyboard beneath the

counter, out of sight, and I exhale. He keys in my information. "What phone number do you have a question about, Ms. Bensen?"

The way he says it, like I have another one on file, is curious. I barely stop myself from asking. "I don't have it memorized."

"303-222-1018," Liam supplies from memory.

"You remember it that easily?"

"I'm a numbers guy."

The mental image of all those numbers trailing from his belly button down to some delicious destination I've yet to explore, and never will, thickens my throat.

"Got it," Scott informs us. "What do you need to know, Ms. Bensen?"

"She needs to know if anyone else is on the account," Liam answers.

Scott looks at me for confirmation.

I'm not sure where Liam is going with this, but I'd like to get there sooner than later. "Is there?"

"Nope," Scott answers. "Just you."

"And the bills go to her directly?" Liam asks.

Scott glances at me.

I tell him, "You can speak freely. Please tell him whatever he wants to know."

"The account is paid for a year in advance. Statements do go to you directly, Ms. Bensen, and any extra charges would therefore be payable by you."

"Does the account have a password of any kind?" Liam asks.

Scott punches a key on his computer. "No password set up."

Liam opens the box and takes the phone out. "Walk her through setting it up."

Scott starts speaking, but I tune him out, focusing on Liam. He never intended to return the phone. This was never about things getting too complicated. He held onto my hand just to hold onto me. I let my state of mind and inexperience with a man like Liam make me a little crazy.

He steps closer to me, sweeping a strand of hair behind my ear. "You need the phone," he says softly. "Set up the password. You can change it at any time." He glances at Scott. "And she can change her number if she needs to as well, correct?"

"Yes," Scott agrees. "If there's a reason she needs to change it, she just needs to call in and provide account validation."

Liam leans down, his hand settling possessively on my waist, branding me. I want to be branded by this man. "If you ever really want to get rid of me," he whispers, "you can always change your number."

He didn't believe my lie. I didn't, either.

A FEW MINUTES later, I've tucked my cell phone into my pocket and let Liam hold the door for me to exit the store. Pausing, I wait for him to join me, instinctively scanning the sidewalk illuminated by moonlight and street lanterns.

"How about that dinner?" Liam asks, stepping beside me, and just that easily I've forgotten my surroundings and there is only him.

"Earlier," I start, "back at the hotel. When I said that I need to say . . ." I still need to say good-bye, but I can't seem to get the words out.

He steps closer to me, sliding his hand to my face. "If you tell me you don't want to be with me, I will listen. I won't like it, but I'll listen. I need you to know that. But when you say you 'can't' be with me, like some obstacle out of your control is stopping you from seeing me, I'm not going to listen."

I am stunned and happy and confused and freaked out

all at once. It is as if he's reached inside my head and ticked off every possible item on a list of things I could need him to say—but it also means he sees too much. And yet . . . not enough. I've never wanted to bare my soul to anyone, yet I do now to a man I barely know.

"Liam—"

He brushes his lips over mine, and while I have no idea what was going to come out of my mouth, I think this is another case of him saving me from saying something we both might regret. "Let's go eat, baby."

I like how familiar that sounds. How not-alone it makes me feel. "Yes," I whisper, accepting the reprieve I'm certain he's intentionally offered me. "Let's go eat."

His eyes light with approval, his fingers interlacing with mine, and in silent agreement we begin to walk. My mind replays that first time I saw Liam in the airport. Even from across a room, he'd spoken to me. I think of making love to him. I think of him picking me up today from the grocery store, and then kissing me in front of the hotel. I think of every second I've spent with this man, so absorbed that I blink when he stops at a restaurant a few doors down from his hotel.

Suddenly I realize that, for all of my thinking, remarkably, there's one thing I *haven't* had on my mind: Godzilla. I haven't thought about whatever monster is watching or lurking around the corner. Liam did that for me.

He holds the door to the restaurant open for me, and for a moment I just stare at him—this brilliantly talented, amazingly generous man, who epitomizes the phrase "tall, dark, and handsome." And I think I'm crazy—crazy for him. And I'm selfish. So very selfish, because I've been so alone, and now he is here, and I don't know how I can walk away from him.

I don't deserve him—and he absolutely does not deserve me.

ELEVEN

AFTER ARRIVING FOR OUR RESERVATION AT North, a chic modern restaurant with frosty dangling lights and steel-and-glass tables, Liam and I are seated inside a high-backed half-moon-shaped booth that seems to hug us in privacy. Our attractive, blond, twentysomething waitress bats her eyes at Liam as she takes our orders for pasta and salads, clearly smitten with him, but from what I could tell on our arrival, so are most of the females in the place. He, however, is a perfect gentlemen, neither disrespectful nor encouraging to her, casting me warm looks that charm me and seat me at ease.

When the woman reluctantly tears her gaze from Liam's face and departs, a waiter appears with the insanely expensive bottle of champagne Liam has ordered for us. Once the cork has been popped and our glasses are filled, Liam and I are finally alone.

He lifts his glass, his eyes burning hot. "To new friends and lovers."

Goose bumps lift on my skin at the intimacy of his words, ripples of awareness tingling across my chest, down to my belly, and I'm blown away by how easily he affects me. I know the sweetness of his mouth on mine, the perfection of his body intimately molded against me, and what it's like to fall asleep in his arms.

I simply clink my glass against his, unable to repeat his toast back to him.

But Liam waylays my escape as my hand retreats, gently shackling my wrist. He arches a dark brow, silent reproach and yes, challenge on his face. This man challenges me at every turn.

Nerves flutter in my stomach. I have been naked with him, with my fingers laced behind my back, yet I feel more naked now than I did then. But I am so tired of hiding from everything—especially myself. And somehow, hiding from him is hiding from me.

Delicately, I clear my throat. "To new friends and lovers," I repeat.

As I see the approval in his eyes, I suddenly know what feels different about this moment than when we'd been making love, or rather, fucking, as Liam called it. Here, in public, there is no veil of spontaneity to hide behind, and in this moment, there is no lie spoken to deny what is burning between us. *This* is the most intimate I have been with this man.

We sip our champagne and the bubbles blossom in my mouth, both tart and sweet, like this night with Liam. Like everything with Liam.

"Good?" he inquires.

I nod and set my glass down. "It's delicious."

"So are you."

Blood rushes to my cheeks, and I am so far out of my safe zone it's not even funny. Or maybe it is, since I can't stop the nervous laughter bubbling from my lips. "Back in New York, if someone had told me I'd be sitting in Denver, having dinner with a gorgeous prodigy architect–billionaire who was giving me compliments, I'd have suggested they needed medical attention." I reach for my champagne and sip.

He sets his glass down and his hand goes to my leg, sending darts of heat up my thigh. "I am what I am."

Probably due to the champagne, I can't hold back a wistful reply. "That's an enviable trait."

"And that means what?"

I down my champagne, and he arches a surprised brow. I'm pretty surprised myself. I value a tightly controlled tongue. "I don't drink much and I haven't eaten much today, so that probably wasn't smart."

"If it makes you stop being afraid to speak your mind to me, then it was a good choice."

I don't play dumb. I probably have the champagne to thank for that, too. "You're intimidating."

"No. Not to you."

"So you agree you're intimidating."

"To some people, but not to you. I'm not your Godzilla, baby, and we both know it."

"No. No, you aren't. Far from it." I stop and wait. Will he push me for the answers he swears he can wait for?

He doesn't ask. He just arches his brow again, the look in his eyes clearly saying, *Did I pass the test?*

"You really aren't going to ask, are you?"

"I told you—"

"Tell you when I'm ready."

"Exactly." He fills my glass and hands it to me.

"Are you trying to get me drunk?"

"Yes. Then maybe you'll feel ready."

I laugh. "You're very . . . honest."

His thumb strokes my cheek, tender and sensual. "Raw and honest, baby. Remember?"

This is a repeating theme with him, and while I've let guilt make the words about me, I wonder if they are really more about him. "Who made you hate lies?"

"Doesn't everyone?"

"That's a deflection." I know because I'm so damned good at it.

Surprise flickers in his eyes and he sets his glass down. "Money breeds lies, baby. They swim like sharks all around me."

More deflection, but it tells me more about him than perhaps he realizes. And about us. Outwardly we are night and day, but I now know why we felt this instant bond. We each sense what's beneath the surface of the other, and it is the same: everyone he once loved in his world is gone. Everyone who still lives wants something from him.

I reach up and touch his cheek. "I don't want your money."

His hand covers mine. "I know."

"The phone—"

"Was a gift to myself. It gives me peace of mind to know that you're safe." His lips curve. "And maybe you'll even feel a little obligated to answer my calls, though I'm not gambling on that."

No one else in this world shows concern for me, and I don't take it for granted. Regretting the buzz in my head, I set my glass down, done with the wine. "I'm serious, Liam. You spent a lot of money on me. I need you to know that I'm not one of those people—"

He leans in and kisses me. "I do know."

"You didn't let me finish."

"You don't have to. I know you aren't one of those people. I don't let those people in." His voice lowers, roughens. "You're in, Amy."

I am stunned by his absolute statement. "You barely know me."

His lips curve. "I can think of all kinds of ways we can remedy that, both with and without clothing."

My smile mirrors his. "You're very bad."

"I think you like that."

"I don't think I know enough to be sure."

"Then we'd better find out."

I shock myself by saying, "Tonight?"

His eyes gleam with approval. "Oh yeah, baby. Tonight."

Tonight. The word lingers in the air and there is a silent understanding between us in a way I have never shared with anyone. We both know that I've just erased the question of where this night will end, and it won't be with me saying a good-bye we both know I never wanted to say. I'll convincingly feed him the information my file says I should, so he won't look into my background. Lies to protect him that handle the here and now. I'll figure out the later when I have some time alone.

A woman lightly clears her throat and Liam and I reluctantly break apart, our eyes lingering on each other's a moment before our salads are placed in front of us. Beneath the table, Liam's hand settles back on my leg, his thumb stroking my knee, and I feel every caress in my sex. I don't want food. I want Liam.

"Need anything else right now?" the waitress asks.

Liam glances in my direction, giving me a look that says *you're my dinner*, as he replies, "Not right now."

The instant she's gone I scold him. "Liam."

He leans in and kisses me. "Liam, what?"

My mouth goes dry. "You have to behave."

"Always, or just right now?"

"Just right now."

A low laugh rumbles from his chest. "I'll behave, so you can enjoy your meal. I've been here a few times and have never been disappointed."

"Was that when you designed the building downtown?" I ask, not afraid of my questions sparking his questions anymore. I believe now that he'll let me answer what I want to answer. I'll figure out what that means later. Not tonight.

Tonight has been decided. I am with him and the rest of the world does not exist.

"Yes. I stayed in this area for a couple of months."

A couple of months. My vow to focus on just tonight evaporates and I make a pretense of picking up my fork and playing with my salad to hide how crazy my mind is going. Will he be here that long this time? What if I get attached to him, and he goes back to New York? He *will* go back to New York—but I can't visit him there. And the cover story in the file won't be enough to explain why. *Raw and honest.* Why can't I actually have that with just one person in my life?

"Hey," he says softly.

I swallow the knot in my throat and glance up. "Hey."

"What just happened?"

I don't have an answer, so I don't offer one. "How did your meeting go today?"

He studies me a moment, and I don't know what he sees, but it's probably too much. "Better than it should have. They have you to thank for that."

"Why?"

"I've decided to stay around for a while. If I can create something I'm excited about in the process, I'd like to."

"You're staying?"

"Yes. Any problem with that?"

I've proven I don't have coyness or good-bye in me with him. "I won't complain about seeing more of you."

His eyes light. "That's good to hear, considering you were ready to kick me to the curb earlier."

"I wasn't. I just . . ." I need more time to think about what to say to him. "Did they like your design?"

"All but one of the investors, who's a complete prick."

"You like him that much, huh? What don't you agree on?"

"Everything. He still wants the tallest building in existence."

I remember his comment on the plane, and smile. "Is he short?"

He laughs, and it's so warm and wonderful that I could roll around in it like sunshine on a cold day. "Actually, yes. He is."

"Hmmm," I say, pondering. "So what do you think? Will you find a way to compromise with him?"

"Too many people involved want my name and skill attached to the project to *not* try to make this work." He's matter-of-fact, not arrogant. "Two of the biggest financial investors won't arrive until Monday. If I win them over with my design, then it's probably a done deal. I'll need to meet with the engineers and make sure everyone is on the same page, but all in all, I'm probably only a week from a decision."

I know that he's said he's staying, but some part of me

aches for further confirmation. "So I get you for at least a week?"

"I told you, baby. Deal or no deal. I'm not in any rush to leave."

I am too relieved, too emotionally dependent on someone I barely know, and I do not understand why. I have had no one. I have relied on me. What is it about this man that makes me want to lean on him, and is that good or bad?

"Here are your entrees," the waitress announces, and feeling exposed and vulnerable for reasons I can't quite understand, I take the excuse to look away from Liam, as she adds, "I'm sorry you didn't have much time on the salads. The kitchen was a bit fast."

Soon we're sipping more champagne and enjoying our pasta, but I have a raw nerve still bleeding vulnerability I cannot seem to seal. Reflexively, I launch into my standard question-asking strategy meant to prevent question answering. Easy to do with Liam when I crave every detail I can learn about him. "Will you tell me about how you started apprenticing in architecture at such a young age?"

"The real story or the one I tell the media?"

I lift a bite of pasta to my lips. "I'll take both, please."

"I had a feeling you would. Alex met me at a public event and learned of my interest in architecture, and took me under his wing."

"And the real story?"

"What makes you think that isn't it?"

"Is it?"

His jaw hardens. "No. The real story is that I was obsessed with drawing buildings, and I told my mother I wanted to be a famous architect."

"How old were you when this started?"

"I was six. At thirteen, I was trying to teach myself from books. My mother heard Alex was in the city to unveil a building, and despite working two jobs, she found a way to get me there. We were living in the Bronx. When I met Alex, he saw something in me." He goes on to tell me about going to Alex's house for weekends and summers.

Until this moment, I hadn't let myself connect the dots of Liam's past to mine. I, too, had been a child protégé, to my gifted father, and I reach for my champagne to keep the confession from falling from my lips. That was my old life— my *real life*.

Amy Bensen has a business degree. She doesn't have a famous archeologist for a father. *My* father is dead.

"Alex tortured me with hours upon hours of math equations," he continues, and I set down my glass, saved from my past by my interest in his.

"I hate math." Although his tattoo could make me change my mind. I grin at the thought. "You seem rather fond of it."

His eyes gleam with understanding. "Alex used to tell me there were infinite possibilities in life and architecture. The tattoo represents that to me."

Infinite possibilities? I'm not sure I like that idea. How many people will I be before I die?

"Of course," Liam adds, "as a kid I just wanted to draw buildings. Alex said that's what you call an artist, not an architect. I fought the math, and ended up doing the whole wax on, wax off thing."

I laugh. "Like in *The Karate Kid*? That was to learn karate. What does that have to do with math?"

"It's hard work—my punishment for not getting the math right and complaining about having to try." He laughs, but it's laced with sadness. "And he liked the movie." He shifts out of the past to the present. "I don't like the movie. I do, however, like math now—funny how mastering something makes you change your tune about it. By the time I was in college, I was a whiz."

The waitress takes my plate, and I am surprised to realize it's empty. A few minutes later we're enjoying coffee and I sigh in contentment, more relaxed than I've been in a very long time.

"What did your parents think about Alex?" I ask, not ready for this dinner to end.

"My mother adored him."

"And your father?"

His expression turns somber. "He wasn't around to have an opinion."

"I want to ask—but I'm not sure I should."

He gives me a wry smile. "And that's about as honest as it gets."

He's right. It is, and it feels good. But what I sense in him does not. "Do you want to tell me?"

"He ran out on us when I was eight," he says easily. Almost too easily. "Told me he was going to the store and never came back."

"You grew up poor." There is so much more to this man than "billionaire architect." "That's why your mother worked two jobs."

"Yes. Until Alex came along. He took care of my mother."

"Were they romantically involved?"

He gives a quick shake of his head. "No. They were just close friends. When she was diagnosed with cancer, Alex paid for her treatment."

I blink. "Cancer?"

"Cervical. She didn't have the money for regular checkups, so it was caught late, but she beat it twice."

My throat thickens. *She didn't beat it the third time.* "How old were you?"

"Fifteen. Alex adopted me."

"Alex lost his child, and you lost your parents."

"Yes. Exactly."

"And Alex? You said you lost him, too?"

"He had a heart attack while I was chasing pyramids a couple of years back." He looks away and reaches for his coffee.

Not knowing what to say, I just sit there until his gaze meets mine again. And I see the truth in his eyes. "You never talk about this."

"No."

"But you did with me."

"Yes. Now ask me why."

"Why?"

"Someone has to go first."

It's his offering of trust, and I know I was right. There is something happening between us, something I may never experience again and ironically that means lying. This is my chance to tell him Amy Bensen's story, to make sure he doesn't dig around on his own.

I open my mouth to relate my fake life per the file, then snap it shut with a stunning realization: Amy Bensen's story *is* Liam's story. Her father ran out on her when she was a kid, and her mother died of cancer. How can this be? It's impossible. I'm not telling this lie to Liam. I can't. I won't.

"I need to go to the ladies' room," I say, and scoot out of the booth with my purse.

But Liam has gotten out on the other side and is standing in front of me, worry in his eyes. It's as if he senses my instinct to bolt. He thinks I'm running away, and I am—but not from him. I'm running from the me I don't even recognize as me.

"Amy—"

I lean into him and stand on tiptoe, brushing my lips over his. "I still want to lick your tattoo. Remember?"

But he doesn't laugh. He gives me an intense look. "Hurry back and let's get out of here."

"Yes. I'd like that."

His hands slowly leave my waist, and I like that he doesn't want to let me go. I have to find a way to make this work.

The waitress directs me to the bathroom, where I rush inside the farthest stall from the door and lock myself inside. I'm back where I was two nights ago, leaning on a bathroom door and fretting. But this time Liam has found me, and I don't want to lose him, or put him in danger. Lies will protect him, and I should embrace them and him while he's in Denver. But deep down, I feel this man inside me—and I don't want to limit our possibilities.

The air shifts in the bathroom and I freeze. I didn't hear

the door open, but I hadn't heard it at the museum, either. My hand goes to my throat and I don't dare breathe. I listen, but don't hear anything. I can't seem to make myself move. What if I leave the stall and there's another note? What if I have to run again?

The cell phone in my purse starts to ring, startling me. Liam—how long have I been standing here?

I shake myself and open the stall door, steeling myself for whatever I find. Rounding the corner to the sink, I stop in my tracks with surprise.

"Meg? What are you doing here?"

She whirls around from the sink, her long blond hair a contrast to her short red dress. "Oh my gosh. Amy! What are *you* doing here?"

"I . . ." My phone starts ringing again.

"Oh, good." She lights up. "You got your phone working. I can't believe we're both here."

"I . . . yes. Very small world."

"That's what I love about this little area of Cherry Creek. You can live, eat, shop, and play here, and get to know everyone like it's a small town. Only we have Chanel and Gucci in our small town. Not that I can afford that kind of thing, but maybe I'll find me a sugar daddy."

Inside, I cringe. While her comment is playful, Liam

must have to deal with real money-chasers. "Are you on a date?"

"My boss brought me. And he's certainly a hot property. What about you?"

"Yes, a date. Who I should get back to."

She pulls her phone out of her purse. "Let me grab your number before we forget."

I can't get out of this. Dang it. I remove my phone from my purse, glance at the numbers on the screen, and my throat goes dry.

Only the first call was from Liam.

The other is unknown.

TWELVE

I STARE AT THE SCREEN, MY mind racing. It has to be a wrong number. No one has this number but Liam—not even my handler. At the thought, my mind flashes back to the one time he called me.

The phone is ringing and I jerk upright in bed. There's no one left to call me—no one I love. But maybe this is all a mistake, and someone is alive! I grab the receiver, my hand shaking so hard I nearly drop it. "Dad?"

"Listen and listen carefully, Amy," a stranger says. "They're coming for you. Get dressed and get the hell to the back door of the hospital. I'll be in a cab waiting for you."

"What? Who are you?"

"There isn't time. Get the hell out of the fucking bed. Now!"

"Okay, ready," Meg announces. "What's the number? I'll type it in so I don't lose it."

I blink through spots, and damn it, my eyes are prickling and my forehead pinching.

Meg is holding her phone up expectantly.

"Right," I croak and try to smile. Somehow, I lift my phone and read the number to her.

If she notices I'm rattled, she doesn't show it. "Great! I'll call you tomorrow and we'll make a date."

"Sure. Yes."

She heads toward the door and I follow her into the hallway, where she has halted, a stunned look on her face. Liam is leaning on the wall, looking to her, I'm sure, like some magazine model or romantic hero who's miraculously popped out of the pages of a novel. His eyes meet mine and I feel the connection inside and out. To me, Liam is what he's been since our plane ride: salve on an aching wound.

He pushes off the wall the instant he sees me and pulls me to him. "I was worried about you."

"He's with you?" Meg asks from behind me, shock in her voice. I refuse to read into it.

Liam answers, "Yes. I'm with her."

Meg whistles and I turn in his arms, comforted by the way his hand settles on my stomach and pulls me back against his chest. "Amy, honey," Meg declares, "I need to know where you shop. I'll call you tomorrow."

She goes down the hallway and I stare after her, fighting the urge to follow her so I can ask her boss about my new boss.

"She'll call you tomorrow?" Liam asks, and I turn to him.

"She's the secretary at the leasing office. She wants to do coffee, or drinks." My hand settles on the hard wall of his chest, and his warmth travels through my body.

"Then why do you look like you saw a ghost?"

I laugh, but it sounds choked. "I guess ghosts are like lies. They swim like sharks all around me." The joke holds so much truth that I'm shocked I allowed it past my lips. I'm even more shocked that I don't regret it.

His eyes are probing, but he doesn't ask any questions. "Sharks only have the power you give them, baby. Own them. Don't ever let them own you. And they'll have to fight me to get to you, anyway."

Suddenly I'm swimming in one part fantasy, one part wicked, hot desire. His declaration stokes my need for him to a full-on fire. And while his words might be pure seduction, I choose the fantasy—the escape he is for me, in a way no one else ever has been.

He leans in and presses his mouth to my ear. "I'm going to take you to my room now, and fuck you until neither of us can walk anymore." His blue eyes blaze in the dim hallway. "Any objections?"

"No," I whisper, and am shocked at how unabashedly I reply to his wicked declaration. "No objections whatsoever." Not only do I want him; he will also make me forget the phone call. He can make me forget everything but him.

"Then let's get out of here." He caresses a path down my arms, raising goose bumps on my arms and I am anything but cold. In fact, the only time I am not cold is in this man's presence. His fingers entwine with mine, and the intimate act of hand-holding that's rapidly becoming familiar creates a burn in my chest. And a moment of fear. I could get used to this. I could get used to him in my life, by my side.

Entering the dining room, I am momentarily jerked back into the world where he is not all there is and where the ghosts that swim like sharks at my feet, and in my head, live. I scan for Meg and her boss, but I don't see them. Relief washes over me. I don't want to think of anything right now but Liam's wicked promise.

THE WALK TO the hotel is silent. The air between us is both electric and soothing, a contrast that speaks to my soul. This is what I need. *He* is what I need. I refuse to let anything else in. I will not melt down in a haze of loss and heartache, or fear over a phone call. I can worry about that tomorrow. In Liam's room I am safe, and in his arms my escape will be complete.

And when we approach the entrance of the hotel, I do not even make a pretense of my mockery of a story about fearing how I will look to the hotel staff. Maybe I should care for other reasons. Maybe I should fear being noticed, and with Liam, it is impossible not to be noticed, but I do not. I am *with* Liam and I will not be any other way in this moment of time.

"Mr. Stone." The doorman greets Liam with a nod.

Liam inclines his head and I drink in his profile, so strong, so confident. I envy him, this man who knew what he wanted to be in life and made it happen. This man who knows where he has been, and who he is.

I know nothing of me—not where I have truly been, or why I'm here. Why I exist. We are not alike, although I'd thought so in the restaurant. We are totally different—but when I'm in his arms, I don't have to face these things, or myself.

The short walk to the elevator feels eternal, and the wait for its arrival even longer. When the doors finally open Liam seems to feel the same urgency, pulling me into the car and pressing me against the wall, his big body framing mine.

My hands go to his chest as he slides a card into the slot for the penthouse, then flattens a hand on the wall above my head. Our eyes connect, and I feel it clear to my toes. Still, we don't speak, as if we're both afraid the spell will be broken and we will be back to good-bye.

When the doors ding open he laces his fingers with mine, tugging me along as if he fears I'll change my mind. After my flip-flopping, I don't blame him, but that is over. I crave the hot, dominant way I know he'll take me away. I want to be here, with him.

A quick swipe of his key card and the door to his suite is open, and he flips the light on as we go inside. I smile as we step toe-to-toe, his hands on my shoulders. "Any second thoughts?" he challenges.

"About how this night started, yes. About now, none."

"Do you want to talk about how it started?"

"Do we have to?"

"No." He takes my hand and starts backing down the hallway, and I willingly follow.

Until the sound of my phone ringing freezes me in place. Urgency feels like lightning in my blood, my future seeming to hang on the unanswered call.

"I have to get this." I tug my hand from his and pull my purse from my shoulder, unzipping it with obviously shaking hands.

Unsteady from panic, I lean against the wall and quickly press Answer before I miss the call again, my heart about to explode as I croak, "Hello?"

"Ms. Bensen?"

"Yes."

"Oh, good," a slightly familiar male voice replies. "This is Scott from the phone store. You left your driver's license here. We close in an hour, if you want to swing by."

Relief washes through me, and my laughter is too close to hysteria. "Thank you. I'll come by tomorrow and get it."

"I'll hold it at the register to keep it safe. Goodnight."

"Thank you again. Goodnight." I end the call and look at Liam, the look in his eyes says I'm in for another game of dodgeball I do not want to play. "I left my ID at the phone store." I step forward to wrap my arms around his neck and mold my upper body to his, warmth spreading from every place we touch. "Where were we?"

His hand splays between my shoulder blades, a hot branding I welcome, but the warning that follows is icy water dousing the fire. "You aren't going to pretend that what just happened didn't happen. Just like you aren't going to tell me you didn't walk into the bathroom at the restaurant running from me, and then exit running from someone or something else. And I'm not buying that it was Meg."

"New places make me nervous." I press my lips to his.

His hand tangles in my hair and gently pulls my head back, forcing my gaze to his, and his eyes are as hard as his voice. "Raw and honest, Amy. That's what we are, or we're nothing at all." He cages me against the wall with his arms, pinning me in a stare. "Tell me who's scaring you, Amy, and I promise I will make them go away."

If only it were that easy. If only he could be my Prince Charming, my hero. But in reality, heroes die, just like everyone else in my life.

I grab his shirt and lean into him. "What happened to fucking me until we can't walk anymore? That's what tonight is supposed to be. Not you making me a mathematical equation you have to crack. I don't want to be cracked, Liam. I don't want to answer questions. I want to be fucked." I barely recognize the woman who can say such a thing. "You promised. You said you were—"

I yelp in surprise as he picks me up and starts walking. "What are you doing?"

"Agreeing with you. No more questions."

Blood rushes to my ears as he carries me through a fancy living room toward the bedroom. That's what I asked for. Actually, I demanded to be fucked. Until last night, I'd never even used the word. This man is changing me, and I'm not sure if that's good or bad.

We enter the bedroom, where a light glows dimly, but he bypasses the bed, setting me on my feet in front of a massive bathroom I barely glimpse before he shuts the door. His intense edginess has cranked up several notches. Is he mad, or . . . hurt? By me? He is confident and experienced and I am . . . whatever I am, but I am less, if I have hurt this man who has already proven he is so much more than his Wikipedia page.

"Liam—"

"No more talking." His hands come down on my waist, a possessive branding, and his voice tight. He walks me backward until my heels hit the bathroom door and I lean against the hard surface. His legs shackle mine, holding me as captive as the burning deep in his eyes. "You want me to fuck you, Amy, I'll fuck you."

Suddenly the word *fuck* feels like a slap, given his mood. "Yes, I do, but—"

His mouth comes down hard on mine, hot with demand, with anger. I don't want him to be angry, and I lean into him, hoping it will fade, hoping to get lost in him, but it doesn't work. I taste the bite of his mood, the roughness of his tongue, and I shove at his chest. "Wait. Not like this."

"You want to fuck or you don't. I'm not a yo-yo any more than you are one of my mathematical equations."

"Don't say it like that."

"Don't challenge me to fuck you and then run away."

Run away. I am always running away and sick of that being my life. "You're just—you're you, Liam, like you said, and I'm . . . me. And you're like a bull when you want something. You charge."

"What I want is you."

Even though I know this, hearing it stirs a sweet spot in my belly. And all I want to do is savor the sensation, and the man who created it. "Then please, just be with me. Just be with me, Liam."

He wraps his fingers around my neck and pulls me to him. "I understand wanting to block things out. Been there, done that—but I won't let you do it to me, baby. We're going to talk tomorrow, but tonight, we'll forget." He brushes his lips over mine, and I tremble from the simple but powerful touch. "Now. Turn around."

He doesn't give me time to respond, and turns me to face the door, my hands against the hard surface, and I'm beginning to think he likes me like this. I think *I* might like me like this. He leans into me, his body deliciously hard, his breath a warm seduction against my neck as he declares, "No more barriers," and tugs my zipper down, though I don't think he's talking about clothes.

I was fooling myself to challenge him to "fuck" me, to think sex is my sanctuary when I'm headed deeper into this web of intimacy with him, a place where he'll want—and even deserve—answers to all of his questions. But as he glides my dress down my shoulders, leaving goose bumps in their wake, I find it hard to care. Already, I'm sinking into the sweet oblivion of pleasure that only Liam has ever helped me find. He is my sanctuary from everything else. He alone is my escape.

"Step," he commands, and I lift my feet one after another and let him toss my dress away. I squeeze my eyes shut when he unhooks my bra, and I shrug out of it, and just like that I'm naked before this man again, my breasts swollen and heavy, my nipples tight, aching with need. His hands flatten on the wall by my head, but he doesn't touch me. He likes this, I think. To trap me. To be in control. And I like it. I like him being in control, instead of the world outside. I like that when I hand control to him, there's pleasure, not pain.

"Turn back around," he commands, and I like that, too. The roughness of his voice, the absoluteness of him being in charge. I face him, and his gaze does a hot up-and-down of my naked body that sizzles every nerve ending I own.

"Take off the shoes."

I kick them off.

"Now the panties and the thigh-highs. I want nothing between us."

But he's fully clothed. "Are you . . . ?"

"When you ask questions, I ask questions."

I swallow hard at the pointed remark. He knows that's what I do. He knows I play dodgeball, and with anyone else it would work. With him, I've already run out of rope. I shove aside the worry and focus on tonight. An escape. With him.

I roll down my thigh-highs and toss them away, and then my panties. I am naked before this man but I am so much more. I'm exposed, vulnerable, somehow I feel protected and safe.

"On your knees," he orders softly.

"My knees?"

"No questions, baby. You do what I say."

I inhale and hold in the air. I trust Liam. *I trust* Liam. When was the last time I said that about anyone?

I lower myself to my knees, the soft carpeting padding my bare skin. Liam squats in front of me. "Hands over your head and on the door handle."

This time I gulp. I can't believe I am doing this, but I do. I curl my fingers around the knob above my head and now I'm truly exposed, my breasts thrust high, my body stretched out for his viewing. But he doesn't look at my body. He searches my eyes, an intense, inscrutable look on his handsome face.

He loosens his tie, then pulls it from his neck. Adrenaline surges through me with the certainty that his shirt and pants are next, but he reaches over to my wrists—and I gasp, realizing that he's using his tie to bind my arms over my head.

I am more than naked and vulnerable. I am at his mercy.

THIRTEEN

WILLINGLY TIED TO THE DOOR, I'M surprisingly without fear, and there's a burn in my belly. The air-conditioning teases my nipples, a striking contrast to the heat in Liam's gaze as it rakes over my body. The tie is snug on my wrists, ensuring I can't escape whatever he intends for me. And anticipation is liquid fire between my thighs; I don't *want* to escape what he intends for me. I am aroused, wet, and aching with an emptiness only he can fill.

It is beyond erotic to allow him this control, and I suddenly realize why his control pleases me. When I'm with him like this, I don't have to calculate what comes next. *He's* doing that.

Finally he begins to undress, and I'm spellbound by this powerful, sexy man, downright hungry to see him completely naked, stripped down in all his masculine glory, a pleasure I didn't have the night before. There was just us ripping whatever clothes off we could to come together. This time is slower, more luxurious.

He toes off his shoes and removes his jacket, then unbuttons his shirt as I impatiently watch. Adrenaline pours through me as dark, springy hair peeks out from behind the fine material, and when his shirt is finally gone, my mouth goes dry at the sight of taut skin over flexing muscle. His hand goes to his pants, and I don't breathe again until he is fully naked, his thick erection pulsing thickly in front of him.

I take in the sight of him, tall and finely carved, he is the definition of masculine beauty, but I hone in on my obsession, one that I am sure many women have shared. The tattoo. My gaze tracks the path of the equation that trails down, down, down, and I swallow hard at where it ends. Liam has singlehandedly made math sexy.

He turns away and my heart thunders in my chest as he opens a dresser drawer, and my heart pounds as I anticipate what he might produce. Tied to a door, I'm sure I should be more afraid. What if it's a whip or chains, or . . . what do people do when they tie up a lover?

He pulls out a box of condoms, and I suddenly feel excruciatingly insecure, aware that there have been many women before me, few men before him.

He tears open the package, and I drop my head to hide my emotions. I'm not sure why this is affecting me this way, but I feel I'm in way, way over my head. I'm probably not even his first bathroom-door affair. Maybe this very tie has been around another woman's wrists. I don't know what to do or say, or how to be. I don't even know my own name half the time. I'm not—

Liam squats in front of me, and the sight of his strong thighs and thick erection cuts off my rambling thoughts. I struggle to regain my composure and re-create some version of Amy that's worthy of this man, even if I, myself, am not.

His finger slides under my chin, and he meets my gaze. "I bought the condoms today, for us, if that's what you're wondering. I don't have women in my hotel room every night. I don't have women in my room—or let them inside my life—at all. Only you."

He reads me like an open book I thought I'd shut years before. "Me," I whisper, reminded of his declaration that *we are raw and honest, or we are nothing.*

"You," he agrees. "And us."

I've never been a part of an "us," and the idea caresses my raw nerves with possibilities. I wet my suddenly dry lips, and Liam leans in and brushes his mouth over mine before he murmurs, "And *we* need to get you on the pill."

"That takes weeks to be effective," I whisper wistfully, something I can't seem to control any more than my feelings or reactions to Liam.

He cups my face and kisses me softly, and I feel myself relax inside. This is what gets to me—the way he's so tender, yet so dominating. It works for me. *He* works for me. So does the way he's trailing kisses over my jaw, teasing my neck, then my ear. "Until then," he says, all velvet and seduction, "I'll be fantasizing about the moment when the only thing wrapped around me is you."

My sex clenches, slickness gathering on my bare thighs. No woman knows what she's been missing until she has a man like Liam say such wicked things to her.

He leans back, his blue stare probing, intimate. "Have you ever been bound before?"

I laugh and the sound is nervousness personified.

He doesn't laugh. His hands frame my face. "And you let me tie you up." There's a husky rasp to his voice that tells me he's affected by this realization.

"Yes," I confirm.

His hand reaches behind me, cupping my backside, and he pulls me to him. His shaft settles between my thighs, and I soften instantly against him. "And I'm just barbaric enough to like being the first in many things."

He said something to this effect before, and it's just as arousing now. "You seem to have a bit of a liking for the word *teacher*."

He caresses up my back and closes his hand on the back of my head, pulling me to him, his cheek finding mine, his voice low and raspy as he murmurs, "I haven't even begun to start teaching you, Amy. We haven't even begun to go where I plan to take you." He drags his lips over my jaw and his mouth lingers a breath from mine. "You trusted me with your body by letting me bind you. I'm going to make sure you don't regret it. That's step one, baby."

His sensual purr on "baby" does funny things inside me, and his lips begin to trail over my jaw, teasing me with the promise of a kiss that I hope soon will follow. And it does. His mouth finds mine, a feather-light touch, a lick of his tongue. I moan with the barely-there, teasing taste of him.

"I like those little sounds you make," he murmurs, rewarding me with another brush of his tongue against mine.

I moan again, ultrasensitive to all that he does to me. He finally deepens the kiss, taking me to that sweet spot where only he exists. *This* is what I want; to be lost in him. I arch into him, craving that connection. Seeming to answer my plea, Liam moves forward, cradling me more fully on his lap, and his hands are all over me, teasing me, driving me wild. The need to touch him spirals through me and I tug at my hands, but there's no escape. There's only the growing ache of need inside me.

His lips leave mine and I reach for his mouth, only to be denied by the bindings on my wrists. "Untie me. I need to touch you."

He frames my face with his hands, and I need them to be other places. Lots of other places. "You're not ready to be untied."

"Yes. I am."

"What are you thinking about right now?"

"I . . . I don't know."

"The first thing that comes into your head. Don't censor it, just say it. Now. What are you thinking of now?"

"Your tattoo."

"Anything else?"

"Touching you."

"And?"

"Ripping the tie off my arms."

He lowers his forehead to mine and his hands brush my breasts, tease my nipples. "And now?"

"How much I don't want you to stop."

"That's the idea. Escape, baby. The lack of control *is* control. When you're hanging on each moment, anticipating what comes next, it leaves room for nothing else. That's what I want to do for you."

I think of his comment about sharks. "And who helps you escape, Liam?"

"We're going to the same place, Amy. I'm not standing outside, watching." His lips find my neck and then my ear. "I'm right here with you."

I close my eyes, luxuriating in the stroke of his hand down my back and his seductive words: *Right here with you.* The promise shimmers down my spine and settles deep inside me. Liam *is* with me. In a tiny amount of time, he has slipped past every wall I've erected.

"Look at me, Amy."

I open my eyes at his soft command, and feel a punch in my chest when my eyes meet his. I'm going to fall hard for this man. I already have.

He leans in and kisses me, pressing my breasts together, then drags his mouth down to my chest to laves his attentions on my nipples, fulfilling a wish I so desired. I suck in a breath at the wet heat as he moves from one swollen tip to the other, mercilessly licking, nipping, teasing until I can take no more.

"Liam, enough. *Please.* I need—"

"What I say you need," he finishes, his hands cupping my backside, lifting my belly to his mouth, dipping his tongue in my belly button, then licking all the way to my hip bone. Nipping the sensitive flesh, licking again.

"Liam, damn it," I pant. I never curse, but I've never been this undone. "You're making me insane!"

He smiles. "That's the idea."

My quaking body disagrees. "No. No, it's not. Pleasure is the idea."

His eyes dance with way too much satisfaction for me to believe he's done tormenting me. "I thought that's what I was providing. Let's see. How about this?" He lowers his head and licks my clit, and I gasp, then whimper as he swirls his tongue several times. He teasingly asks, "Is that pleasure?"

I squeeze my thighs around his shoulders. "Stop tormenting me."

He blows on my clit. "It's called foreplay."

My lashes flutter, but I manage to glare at him. "No, it's—"

His mouth closes on me, and waves of pleasure ripple through me. I tug at my hands, desperate to hold his head, to make sure he doesn't stop this time. His fingers slide inside me, stretching me, caressing me. And his tongue, his amazing tongue, is both sandpaper and silk, stroking me to the edge, then masterfully soothing the ache. Over and over he licks me to the edge of bliss, then pulls back.

"Liam!" I gasp. I'm trembling with how close I am, needing him to give me relief, but he does not.

He leaves my clit and slides his torso up my body, settling his cock thickly between my thighs, his searing stare meeting mine. "We come together."

He presses inside me, stretching me, filling me, and I can barely breathe from the pleasure. I'd wanted the sweet bliss his tongue promised, but now *this* is what I want.

He holds us there, his hands firmly on my hips, his shaft deep in my sex, and challenges me with, "What do you want, Amy?"

"Everything," I pant. "You. I want you."

His eyes darken and he leans in, bringing our mouths a breath apart. "Everything?"

It is a question and a demand, and in this moment—perhaps in every moment since I met him—there is only one answer. "And more."

He doesn't move. There's a spike of energy between us, like a craving unsatisfied. "More," he echoes before he kisses me, and I taste the same burn in him, the same need. He molds me closer, arching into me, and begins to pump his hips. Then there's just the wild passion consuming us, and he is touching me, moving inside me, and I'm going crazy with my hands tied. I want to touch him. I *need* to touch him.

He's on edge too, his grip tightening around my hips, his face buried in my neck. With a guttural moan he pushes harder, deeper, and my sex is one deep pulse around his shaft, the source of a wave of pleasure that spreads through my entire body. I am falling, tumbling, and finally, I crash into that sweet spot. He pumps into me again and I feel a shudder run through his body, or maybe it's me who is shuddering as we melt into one another.

He reaches up and unties my hands, and my arms fall around his neck. Liam shifts us and strokes the hair from my eyes. "We aren't anywhere near finished. You know that, right?"

"Promise?"

"Oh, yeah. I promise. And I never make a promise I don't keep."

He shifts his weight and somehow stands up with me still wrapped around him, him still inside me. I bury my face in his neck, inhale the scent of him, the prickling of memories trying to surface fading into his words earlier tonight. *Tell me who's scaring you and I promise you, Amy, I will make them go away.* Or they will make him go away. I can't let that happen.

I WAKE TO the soft rumble of Liam's voice nearby, and I smile with the realization that I didn't have a nightmare last night—thanks to Liam, who spent the night with his big body wrapped around mine. His big, sexy body, I amend. I am sated and relaxed. *Safe.* I feel safe with him.

Rolling over in the big, comfortable bed, I watch the curtain flutter over the open sliding glass door a few feet away, confirming Liam's location. "I'm not meeting with him today, Derek," I hear him say, sounding more than a little displeased. "Forget it. I have plans I'm not giving up for that jackass. Monday." A pause. "Yeah, well, he's lucky I'm motivated to stay around Denver for a few months. And no. That's none of your business."

Motivated to stay around Denver for a few months. I revel in these words, savoring them. But he'll eventually return to New York, *where you can never go again*, I remind myself. Eventually he will be gone.

"Good morning." He has parted the curtain and is standing in the doorway, dressed only in blue pajama bottoms.

I sit up, hugging the sheet to myself, but I'm not shy in my inspection of his body. I gobble up every detail of this hot man I've had the pleasure of waking up to, from his lean, hard body to the lightly shadowed jawline that makes his goatee even sexier. "You, Liam Stone, are too good-looking for the safety of womankind. And I probably look bad enough to scare small children and a few animals, too."

He laughs, and it's deep and wonderful and far better than cinnamon rolls in the morning. He starts toward me and I hold up my hand. "Wait. Stay right there."

His brow furrows as he stops, and I can't believe I'm about to do this, but that savor-him-until-he's-gone thing is ripe in my mind. Throwing aside the sheet, I expose my naked body and I don't let the heat of Liam's inspection slow me down. I rush forward and stand in front of him, fully exposed.

Liam arches a brow, a question in the gorgeous blue eyes I could drown in. I answer by dropping to my knees and pressing my mouth to his tattoo, my hands on his lean hips. He sucks in a breath, his body tensing slightly, and I smile. I've surprised him, which pleases me.

My gaze lifts to his, and the heat in his stare empowers me. I lick his stomach with a long, slow stroke, then drag my finger down the line of numbers until it dips beneath his waistband. "Now I'm going to kiss my way down—"

A knock sounds on the door, and Liam groans.

I rise to my feet. "You have company?"

He wraps me in his arms. "Room service. I thought waking you up with breakfast in bed was a good idea—until you started licking my tattoo."

"You were going to wake me up to breakfast in bed?"

"Then make you the second course." Another knock sounds, and he gives me a quick kiss. "Just to be clear. Sexy is me waking up to you in my bed and looking just like you do now, tattoo-licking optional, though not discouraged. Grab one of my shirts. I don't want any sneak peeks from room service. I plan to keep you for myself." He heads toward the other room.

I stare after him. He plans to keep me for himself.

FOURTEEN

FIFTEEN MINUTES LATER WE'RE SITTING AT a table on the balcony, drinking coffee and sampling the enormous amount of food Liam ordered to make sure there was something I liked. What I like is him bare-chested and relaxed in his pajama bottoms, with sexy, mussed-up morning hair. And me in his shirt, with his scent teasing my nostrils.

I pluck a grape from a basket with a variety of fruits, and laugh at his argument that the *Fast & Furious* movies are of cultural importance. "And you support this claim how?"

"The movies were released over the course of more than

a decade. One could say they're an historical biography of the evolution of muscle cars."

"One such as you."

He smiles, and his eyes are as perfect as the bright blue sky above. "One such as me."

I cover my empty plate, which once held a fluffy cheese omelet. "Is there a collection of muscle cars to go along with this interest?"

"No—too impractical. I live vicariously through the movies."

"And here I thought you were a Bentley kind of guy."

"I'm not a flashy guy."

"But you love *The Fast and the Furious*."

"All men love *The Fast and the Furious*."

"But you are not all men, Liam."

His shoves his plate aside and leans close, his elbow on the table. "And why is that, Amy?"

"The obvious answer is, because you're a famous prodigy and a billionaire."

"And if I let those things be who I am, then they're *all* that I am. If those things are stripped away, I'm a man who loves hamburgers, the *Fast and Furious* movies, Thirty Seconds to Mars, and the History Channel, which we've determined we have in common."

I laugh at the way he sums himself up, charmed by the

unexpected randomness of his interests. "And some violinist—"

"David Garrett."

"David Garrett," I repeat, "who you swear will seduce me into loving his music. All these pieces of you are not what I expected."

"Is that good?" His voice is softer now, rougher.

"Yes. Yes, it's good."

"Unexpected and good. Much like us."

I'm surprised, pleased, and warmed in a way the sunshine can't begin to touch. "Yes," I say, sealing my decision to savor these few weeks with this man. "Unexpected." So very unexpected.

"And good," he prods.

I smile. "And good."

His cell phone rings, and he grimaces and hits Decline. "Derek—the guy I was talking to when you woke up. He's an investor in the building project, and the only reason I considered being involved. He gets me and what I do."

"Do you need to go meet with him? Because I'm fine if you do."

"No. They'll wait until tomorrow." He changes the subject. "Do you have a passport?"

My unease is instant; a fizzle of fear in my torso over his motives. I laugh nervously, feeling as if I've been on a casual drive and just got sideswiped. "My travels have been as ambitious as sampling the various cupcake shops around Manhattan."

He smiles, and it's almost as devastatingly sexy as his tattoo. "Sweet tooth?"

"Mammoth-sized, though I don't indulge often, or *I'd* be mammoth-sized." Why did he ask about the passport?

He lifts the cover off a plate to display a chocolate waffle concoction. "I have a sweet tooth, too." He hands me a fork. "I'll dare if you will."

I take the fork and my hand trembles. Liam gently shackles my wrist, and I inhale and look at him. "What's wrong, Amy?"

I want to scream at my complete inability to mask my emotions with him. After that first year of melting down, I've always handled myself smoothly. "I feel like I'm keeping you from work." *Lie. Lie. Lie.*

His eyes narrow and I think he'll call me on my reply, but he doesn't. His hand slides away and he motions to the chocolate goo on the plate. "Shall we?"

"Yes," I breathe out. I spoon up the sugary treat and take a bite.

Liam does the same, watching me. "Good?"

"Yes. Delicious."

"Now we have two things on our to-do list," he says.

"Oh?"

"The doctor," he reminds me, and when I should be worried about the passport reference that seems so bizarre, I instead remember last night. *Until then, I'll be fantasizing about the moment the only thing wrapped around me is you.*

"And the second item?"

"David Garrett is touring in Europe the rest of the year. That's why I asked about the passport. I'd like to take you to a concert." His lips quirk in that sexy way. "I can seduce you in another country."

My tension is replaced by regret. I don't know if I can risk having my identity be scrutinized. "As much as I'd like to go, my job is only certain for a few months. I need to look for something more long-term."

His expression doesn't change, but I sense a sharp shift in his mood. "The job with the boss who provided you with an apartment."

I bristle, something in his tone setting me on edge. "What does that mean, Liam?"

"It's not safe to go to work for a guy you don't know, and who provides you with an apartment. Does he have access to it?"

My pulse races at the concern that mimics my own. "It's my apartment. He just arranged it with a Realtor. I pay for it."

He studies me, and the seconds feel eternal before he says, "There's something about the situation that feels wrong. I'm going to have him checked out."

This is exactly what I feared. The more involved I am with Liam, the more he'll dig into my life. "He's just my boss. And this is just a bridge job. That's the point. I need to focus on finding a permanent one."

"That friend of mine, Derek, runs a large real estate investment firm. I'll introduce you and see if he has anything you might be interested in."

I am not about to apply for work with his friend, who then would have a human resources file on me, but I can't say that. "Thank you."

"And I'm going to pay your rent for a year, so you don't have to stress about it anymore."

Stunned, angry, and hurt, I shove to my feet. "No, you're not." I feel like a charity case, bordering on becoming a tramp. "I'm going to get dressed and leave."

He's immediately in front of me, his hand on my arm with the possessiveness I crave and reject.

I lash out. "I guess I pay you for my rent by fucking you all night until we both can't walk?"

Liam looks stunned. "Where did that come from, Amy?"

"I'm not some kept woman, Liam. You've got the wrong girl."

"'Kept woman'? That's crazy." He softens his voice. "You must know that's not how I am, or how we are."

"How can I not feel like that? I don't want your money, Liam. I don't like how I feel right now."

"It's not about the money . . ."

It's not about the money. I hear nothing else. Spots form in front of my eyes, and a distant, unwelcome memory forces itself on me. I squeeze my eyes shut, trying to block out what I instinctively don't want to see, but the past refuses to be ignored. I'm transported back to a day when I'm excitedly running up the porch stairs of my family home to share my acceptance letter from the University of Texas with my mother. I can see the denim skirt and red tank top I'm wearing, and smell the honeysuckle bushes off the side of our huge wooden porch. I reach for the doorknob to open it, and freeze at the sound of my mother shouting. *It isn't about the money. It was never about money.*

"Amy."

I blink and realize that I'm on the bed with Liam sitting beside me, his hand on my leg, and I don't remember how I got here. "I, ah . . ."

"Blacked out," he says. "You scared the fuck out of me."

"I'm sorry." I sit up and lean against the headboard. "I'm okay." *It's not about the money.* I hear my mother's voice in my head again and drop my face to my hand. I've tried desperately so many times to remember my mother's voice, to hear my mother's voice, to remember the way she used to go around the house singing to the radio.

But not today—not in this partially formed memory that some part of me seems to be clawing to get at, while another part blocks it from entry. Maybe it isn't even real. Sometimes I don't know what is or isn't anymore. I don't know how I can want to know the truth yet fear it this badly.

Liam presses his cheek to mine. "You're okay, baby. I'm here, and nothing is going to happen to you."

My hand goes to his, and I want to tell him it's not me I'm worried about. It's him.

He strokes my hair, gently turning my face to his. "Can you walk to the car?"

The dull throb in my forehead is easing, but I must not be clearheaded yet, because I have no idea what he's talking about. "Car? Where are we going?"

"We need to go to the ER and make sure you're okay."

I stiffen and fight through the clawing sensation in my gut, the aftermath of hearing my mother's voice. "No. It's just cluster headaches. They feel eternal, but they only last a few minutes."

"How often?"

"They went away several years ago, and just started again."

"Have you had an MRI?"

"Yes. I'm fine. They usually can't explain why they happen to sufferers. They just happen. I'm supposed to watch for triggers like stress, change of environment, and what I eat. I'm sure it's the move."

"Do you take meds?"

I shake my head. "There isn't much they can do for them, since they come so fast. Acupuncture helped. They went away for years after I tried it."

"And they just came back today?"

"A couple of days ago."

His hands curve around my calves and he scoots closer. "Nightmares and cluster headaches. Sometime soon, you're going to have to tell me. You know that, right?"

All too well. "Moving here was a big decision, Liam. I've always been like this. Big things mess with me. It goes way back to my childhood nightmares."

"I'll accept that answer for now, as long as you agree to see a doctor."

"I don't need a doctor."

"What if you'd been driving?"

"I wasn't."

"Or walking down the stairs? I'm going to be stubborn on this. You need to see a doctor."

"Acupuncture worked before. I'll find a place to go."

"I think you should be checked out by an MD again, to be safe."

"I'm not spending thousands of dollars for them to run MRIs and tests to tell me what I already know."

"Humor me and see someone. I'll pay for it."

"Stop trying to spend money on me."

"Stop hyperfocusing on the money. This isn't about—"

My head pinches. "Stop. Stop. Don't say it again. I get it. You have money and you spend $100 bills like it's my penny. But I am not wasting it, no matter how much you have. I know what works, and that's acupuncture."

Disapproval furrows his brow. "I'll get you an appointment, but if it doesn't work—"

"It will, and I can get my own appointment."

"But you won't, because you want to save money—which is exactly why I'm going to take some of the pressure off of you. Tomorrow I'm going to the leasing office and pay your rent for a year—"

"No, I told you. I'm not going to take your money."

"It's done, baby. No strings attached. No conditions. If you want to ask for a refund after I pay it, you can donate the money to charity, but I won't take it back. A gift is a gift, and I expect nothing in return. Not even a promise of tomorrow." He leans in and kisses me, and I mean to pull back, but his tongue presses past my teeth for one irresistible, deep, silky caress. "And tomorrow won't be enough," he adds.

"Liam—"

He kisses me again and I lose my thought. "Stop kissing me," I reprimand, sounding completely unconvincing. "You're trying to distract me."

"Is it working?"

"Yes. That's the problem."

"Then why would I stop?" He looks exceedingly pleased with himself.

I press my fingers to his lips. "Please stop throwing money at me."

He covers my fingers with his hand. "I want to do this for you, Amy." His voice softens. "Please let me."

Please let him? My heart squeezes with the sincerity I sense in him, and I reach up and stroke his cheek, the line of his goatee. He is amazing and generous and so much more than I bargained for, in every possible way. "You're new territory to me, Liam. I've never met anyone like you. You're overbearingly generous and overwhelmingly male—or maybe it's the reverse. Sometimes I don't know how to respond."

He pulls me down on the bed and under him. "I'd say I'd show you, but I think we'd better wait, considering you blacked out a few minutes ago."

"I told you, it's over. I'm fine now." I smile. "So show me."

"You're sure?"

Finally, a question I can answer without hesitation. "Yes. Please." Take me away, and block the piece of my past that's trying to claw through me.

IT'S NEARLY ONE in the afternoon, Liam and I are walking through the hotel lobby, and I'm a nervous wreck. I do not even care that wearing the same dress as the night before screams "sleepover" to the hotel staff. I cannot walk away from memories that hold answers, but at the same time my mind rejects even thinking about what that means right now. Not when we're heading to my apartment so I can change clothes before we go to the cellular store and pick up my ID, which is another chance for Liam to find out it's a Colorado license. Before I deal with that potential bombshell, I have to explain why the things I left in New York City haven't been delivered. I hate lying, but when I made the decision to stay with Liam, I made the decision to fully be Amy Bensen.

As we step beyond the awning and into the beaming sunlight, my breath hitches at how exquisitely male he is.

His thick, dark hair is a finger-combed sexy mess. He's dressed in a snug black polo pullover, black jeans, and deck shoes. Half an hour ago, he was exquisite in nothing but droplets of water and the soap that I had the pleasure of lathering him with. I've never showered with a man before. I've never felt like this about anyone before. And I don't want my past to destroy it, as it has every other relationship I've had in my life.

We pause to allow cars to pass before we cross the street to my apartment, and I steal a glance at Liam only to discover him doing the same to me. He smiles a devastatingly sexy smile at me, and pulls me under his arm, melding our hips together. My arm slides around his waist and he leans down and gives me a quick peck on the lips. A sweet, hot spot forms in my chest; this moment speaks to me in a way that all the hot sex can't. Neither of us does relationships, yet that's exactly what it feels like we are doing.

We cross the street without breaking apart, and I have this sense of being sheltered from the storm brewing all around me. I think of the leasing office providing me instructions for my work assignments, and a needling begins inside me. Why would my handler leave anything for me with someone else?

Approaching my apartment door, I dig in my purse for my key and will my nerves to calm down. The "zone" I slide into to perform seems pretty nonexistent where Liam's concerned, but I have to find it now. For his own good.

Somehow, I unlock the door with a steady hand. The walls of my zone are trying to form, but they're as paper-thin as my ability to resist this man. Entering the hallway, Liam is on my heels, but I pause in front of him and flip on the light, taking a deep breath. I turn to wait while he shuts the door, blocking his entry, a soldier drawing a hard line.

He arches a brow, and I really wish he wasn't so damned sexy when he did that. "Don't jump to conclusions," I warn. "The moving company lost my things. I'm filing a claim. I took out the insurance I needed, so I'll have my things replaced, so don't go offering to help. I don't need help."

"It could take weeks to get a check."

"I bought some things to get me by."

He stares down at me with that unreadable mask he wears like a champion poker player. "Show me."

"Show you what?"

"What you have to survive on until you get a check." He drags me with him to the bedroom, opens the door to the empty closet, and actually glares at me as if I've done something wrong. "What exactly did you buy to get through the delay?"

"It's not your business to—"

"I'm making it my business." He walks to the dresser, opening all the drawers and removing the few items I purchased yesterday, setting them all on the bed. "This is what you call getting by?" He looks at a price tag and grimaces. "A couple of outfits from the bargain racks and not much else?"

My defenses prickle. "I'm not spending money I don't have to."

He sits down on the bed, pulling me between his legs, his fingers playing on my hips, his mouth pressing to my belly. It's so unexpected that my mood softens instantly, and I almost forget how overbearing he's being. "Change clothes and let's get out of here," he says softly. "I don't like this apartment, or you being in it."

My suspicion over him not pushing me on the purchase of more clothing takes a backseat to other questions. "What's wrong with this place?"

"Aside from preferring you in my hotel and my bed, I don't like the setup of a boss you've never met arranging your lease."

He's turning the pages on my cover story far too quickly. "Lots of employers line up housing when employees relocate."

"Not for one they only intend to keep for a few months."

"My ex-boss is good friends with him. And all he did was contact his Realtor to find me something."

"Are you certain he's not on the lease and has no access to the apartment?"

That hits a nerve. "Of course he doesn't have access."

"Nevertheless, I'm going to get your locks changed."

"You can't just decide to change my locks, Liam," I say, despite that being exactly what I intend to do. I have to reel him in before he pries into things that get him into trouble. "You can't take over my life, Liam."

"I'm not asking for a key."

"No. You'd just take one. And this isn't about a key. It's about you being overly bossy."

His hands slide under my dress, up the back of my thighs. "You like it when I'm bossy."

"Only sometimes." Too often, and I fear it speaks to how much I'm breaking down again. "Those times usually include us not wearing clothing."

He smiles. "Just stay with me at the hotel. Problem solved."

My desire to agree is so intense, it's frightening. Too easily he could leave, and I'd be broken and alone again. "I need to stay here and start making this home."

A knock sounds on the door, and I tense before I can stop myself.

"Expecting someone?" Liam asks.

"I don't know anyone to expect," I tell him, my mind racing.

Who would visit me, except maybe my handler? I haven't even checked for e-mail, and the possibility that I've missed something important sets my heart leapfrogging.

I flash back to the call in the hospital. *They're coming for you.* If they come for me, they could come for Liam, too.

FIFTEEN

I WALK SILENTLY TO THE DOOR and look through the peep-hole, relieved to see Jared leaning casually on the doorframe, wearing a pale blue T-shirt with a Boeing logo.

When I open the door, he straightens. "Hey," he says with a sexy smile I imagine he has down to a science.

That familiar sensation I get with him is back. "Hi."

He holds up an envelope. "This blew off of your door, so I thought I'd hold onto it for you."

As I accept it, I note that it's free of any text or stamps. It's also not sealed. "Thank you."

"It gave me an excuse to check on you." He gives me a half-smile as he adds, "You gave me a scare yesterday. I came by earlier last night but you didn't answer. I was concerned about you being alone, after you almost bit the dust."

"She wasn't alone. She was with me, and what do you mean she almost bit the dust?"

Liam steps by my side, his hand sliding around my waist, and the touch is branding, his hip leaning into mine. The two men's gazes lock and I'm suddenly swimming in a pool of testosterone, in need of a life raft. The crackle of competition, being pushed and pulled is almost palpable.

"Liam Stone," I say, "meet Jared Ryan. Jared lives across the hall—or at least he will for thirty days."

"Thirty days?"

"That's right," Jared says, offering no explanation, the two-word answer hanging in the air with the heaviness of a storm cloud about to erupt. Silence lingers and we all three just stand there.

And stand there. Oh good grief, I'm losing my mind. Someone say something!

"Do you work for Boeing?" Liam asks, proving he isn't done being direct, and I'm curious about the answer as well.

"No," Jared replies. "I have a Dallas Cowboys shirt, too, and I don't play football, either."

Liam looks irritated, while I'm slightly amused. I wonder why Jared is so secretive—maybe he simply doesn't like Liam? Or maybe, like me, he has something to hide. This doesn't sit well.

"Glad you're okay, Amy. If you need anything, you know where to find me." Jared crosses the hall to his door, and looks back as he's about to enter. "I'm in safe, now. You two can go back inside."

I move from the doorway, turning away from Liam, intending to escape to the other room to see what's in the envelope. But Liam shackles my arm. Clearly we are turning the entryway into the confrontation corner of the apartment. "What does he mean, you almost bit the dust?" he demands.

"I hadn't eaten." Truth.

"You had another blackout."

"You're being overbearing." Another truth. I'm liking this confrontation so far.

"Don't be coy," he warns.

I deflect. "What was the 'she's with me' thing all about? I'm not property, Liam." I try to move away, but he blocks me, and I can feel my emotions building inside me, ready to explode. I need to know what's in this envelope. "Let me pass. You're being more barbaric than you are Prince Charming." I can't take it back. It's out, and it's like a rock landing at our feet.

Liam's hands drop away as if I've burned him, and there's no missing the petrified look on his face.

My gut twists in knots. "Stop looking like one of your sharks just bit you."

I head to the bedroom, and this time he lets me. Damn it, I keep turning this into more than it is, but he sends mixed signals. As do I. I lied when I said I wasn't looking for Prince Charming, because deep down, I know I've made Liam my hero. And I know how dangerous that is, for too many reasons to count.

I pause at the bed to grab the shorts and tank top I wore yesterday, then shut myself in the bathroom, setting the envelope down on the sink. The possibility that it might send me racing for another new location is too much to take, and I can't seem to make myself open it. I kick off my heels and tear my dress over my head, then stare at the envelope some more.

"Just get it over with," I whisper and reach for it, flipping open the flap and pulling out a copy of my signed lease with a note attached.

```
I was in your neighborhood and Dermit
wanted me to check on you and drop this
by. Looks like I missed you. Call the
office if you need anything.

Luke Evernight
```

I should be relieved, yet a frisson of unease slides down my spine. Why? What is it that's bothering me?

The bathroom door suddenly opens, and Liam is an un-stoppable force. He lifts me onto the counter, sending the papers in my hand flying to the floor. His arms frame mine, his hands on the counter by my knees.

"Reality check, Amy. I never promised to be Prince Charming."

I flinch. "I told you, I'm not looking for a Prince Charming."

"I fuck and move on."

"You told me that before. I don't want to hear it again."

"The last time I had a long-term girlfriend was in col-lege, and she left me because she said I was self-centered, cold, and just wanted to be between her legs. And it was true, for all kinds of reasons. I am *not* a relationship guy."

"What do you want me to say, Liam? Please fuck me for a few days and move on? I didn't even *say* that word before I met you, but fine! Fuck me for a few days and move on, but stay out of my business. Stop asking ques-tions. Stop trying to change my locks and order me to go to the doctor—just stop. No barbarian routine unless we're naked. Period."

He scrubs a hand through his hair. "I'm not explaining myself well, which shows how out-of-my-skin you make me. My point is that *I'm* the one who's in unfamiliar territory. When I saw that smartass look at you like he wanted to strip you naked, I had to fight the urge to throttle him. I've never felt that before. Never."

"What? No. He—no."

"Yes, he wants you. *I want you.* I can't walk away from you, Amy, and I have this sense that you could bolt at any minute. And you're right: I'm being barbaric. And intense. That's who I am, and I can't be anyone else. When I want something, I go after it. And baby, I want you, and all I can say is you might be smart to run before I get any more into you, but please don't."

His voice is gruff, vulnerable in a way I didn't know he was capable of being. His eyes are blurred with shadows and torment over me, and over something in his past I don't understand.

All I know is that he's letting me see it, and him, and he's exactly what he preaches: raw and honest and intense. We're the same colors, none of them bright or beautiful. We are many shades of gray and black, hoping to find a glimmer of light in each other.

I press my hand to his cheek and he leans into my touch. "I don't want to go anywhere," I whisper. I don't want him to go anywhere, either, but deep down, I know one of us will. We're destined to end. This is the way of my world, and he's as captive to it as I am, without knowing it.

"Then I'm not going to let you," he says, his hand sliding into my hair, his mouth closing on mine, and I taste more than passion. There's the promise that he means to hold onto me, and I pray it's not one we'll both regret.

JUST BEFORE LIAM and I walk into the cell phone store, his phone rings. "It's Derek. I'll meet you inside."

Relief washes over me. He won't see my Colorado license.

As I step into the store I hear him say, "No, I'm not going to meet with him today," followed by a deliciously deep, sexy laugh I could seriously get drunk on.

Scott's talking on the phone behind the counter, and he waves me forward. I'm eager to take advantage of Liam's absence, but the customer on the line seems to be difficult and I find myself knotting my fingers, willing the call to end.

My gaze falls on a typed note about some cell phone accessories, and my mind goes to the typed note left on my door.

I was in your neighborhood and Dermit wanted me to check on you and drop this by. Looks like I missed you. Call the office if you need anything. Luke Evernight.

I straighten. *"Looks like I missed you."* The note was typed, but it sounds like he'd handwritten it, when I didn't answer the door. That doesn't make sense.

Scott hangs up and slides my ID to me. "Here you go, Ms. Bensen. Nice and safe."

I shake myself back to the present. "Thank you. I'm so glad you kept calling. I thought it was a wrong number."

He frowns. "I only called once, when I spoke with you."

"Just once?"

He nods.

"Oh." My throat thickens. So someone else *had* called me. "I received another unknown call. Can you look up who it came from?"

"Unknown or blocked?"

I grab my phone and look. "Blocked. I guess I thought they were the same. Yours was blocked, too."

"No, blocked means you intentionally make sure the person can't find your contact info. I called from my cell, so I blocked the call."

"But no one except you has my number." And Meg, but that was after the unknown calls.

"It's probably overflow from whoever had the number before you."

"Okay. Thank you for everything." I sound calm, but I feel like a wheel spinning out of control. Liam's right. Something *is* off about what's happening around me.

I head toward the door and pull up Gmail on my phone, checking my new in-box. No messages from my boss, or anyone else. Suddenly going back to the apartment feels creepy, and I'm all for going to Liam's hotel tonight. I'll figure out what to do next tomorrow.

I reach the door and Liam holds it open for me, ending a call as he does, and just seeing him brings my tension down a notch.

As we start walking back, he tells me, "I found an acupuncturist who'll come to the hotel this afternoon and do a treatment."

"I didn't even know they worked on Sundays, let alone did house calls."

He winks. "I can be persuasive."

"You have to stop spending money on me."

"Stop thinking of everything like it's money spent. I know that's hard; I had to adjust to it at one point, too. But this is who I am, Amy. You have to get used to it."

I want the chance to get used to *him*.

Liam continues, "Afterward we can order room service, watch movies, and get naked so I can be barbaric in approved territory. Actually, I think I'll call that side of me 'the Beast.' Let's go set him free."

"'The Beast'?" I laugh, and I like that he's confident enough to laugh at himself, and try to find boundaries that work for us both.

"That's right, baby. Let's go get your things from your apartment."

My fear of becoming deeply attached to him and then losing him comes back with force. If I move to his hotel indefinitely, I'll never want to leave.

I stop in the middle of the sidewalk, making people go around us. "Liam. I like that side of you. I like you."

He pulls me against him. "I'm insane for you, Amy. 'Like' lasted all of ten minutes."

"I've been alone a long time," I admit, letting myself be vulnerable. "I'm afraid of forgetting how to be without you." I laugh nervously. "I can't believe I'm telling you this on a busy sidewalk."

He leads me out of the crowd, settling me against a brick wall, his body shielding me from passersby. "How long have you been alone, Amy?"

"Six years." It's out before I remember my documented new story.

"Since you were eighteen."

I nod. "Yes."

"Without anyone else to depend on?"

"Right."

He curses and scrubs his face. "Did you date?"

"I tried in college. My dormmate's legs ended up around my boyfriend's neck and suddenly I was done with the dating thing."

"No wonder you have nightmares and cluster headaches."

"They aren't headaches." I don't mean to blurt it out, but it feels good to tell him. To feel safe enough to let him see a small part of the battle I'm fighting. "That's a lie I tell, so people won't think I'm crazy. They're blackouts and flashbacks."

He kisses me. "That's not a lie, baby. It's survival."

He's right. Surviving is all I've lived for. Until now. Until him.

"How?"

I don't have to ask what he means. I've implied I lost my family all at once. I've promised myself I will lie to protect him to ensure he survives—but not now. "I can't talk about it without crumbling." My eyes prickle, the pain of the past biting a path through my body into my heart, deep into my soul. "I . . . I can't."

He wraps his arm around my neck and lowers his forehead to mine, and if I felt sheltered before, I feel completely protected now, like nothing exists but Liam. "I've had my share of dark days," he confesses. "I get it. You don't have to do or say anything you don't want to."

I surprise myself, and him, by laughing. "I don't have to do anything I don't want to, *except* change my locks, go to the doctor, and let you spend money on me I don't want you to."

He smiles, and it's devastating. "Exactly. Except those things." He motions me forward. "Let's go get your things and then lock ourselves in my hotel room."

SIXTEEN

I WAKE THE NEXT MORNING TO the sound of a cell phone ringing. I'm naked, on my stomach, and Liam's heavy leg is draped over mine.

Liam groans and opens his eyes. "If I ignore it, it will end."

I laugh. "But it will ring again. And don't you have meetings?"

"The alarm hasn't gone off. I'm not leaving this bed with you one second before I have to." The cell stops ringing, and the alarm goes off. He groans again. "I think I'll call in sick." Then the cell starts ringing again. "Oh, hell."

He rolls over and answers the call, listening a moment and then, "What do you mean, he's not here?" He sits up to lean against the headboard and I lift myself up on my elbows, my gaze riveted by his tattoo—that sexy, wonderful tattoo I could happily wake up to every morning.

"Emergency, my ass," Liam continues. "This is a power play—you know it is. And no, I'm not coming in until he's back. That's his intention. Get me committed to the project and I'll do it his way. I won't. Meeting with anyone else before he and I come to terms is a waste of everyone's time."

I can't help myself. I inch over to Liam and begin kissing his stomach. Liam glances down at me, his eyes simmering with desire, and the sheet begins to lift. I laugh and lick the 3.14 above the pi sign.

"I'm staying—and not because of him," Liam tells the caller. "Call me when he gets back. We'll go from there." He ends the call, tosses the phone onto the nightstand, and drags me up his body before rolling me onto my back.

"Oh, the things I can do to you with a full day in bed." It's a wicked warning and a promise of punishment in the most pleasurable of ways. He proved this to me last night. He'll take me to the edge and make me wait. He'll make me ask for things I never thought I could ask for. But he will make me forget everything but him. And right now, I need him more than answers.

MIDAFTERNOON FINDS LIAM and me downtown on the top floor of a high-rise, snuggled into the cozy chairs of a coffee shop overlooking the site where the new shopping complex is supposed to be built. I'm dressed in black shorts and a red tank Liam has forced me to buy by dragging me into a store, slapping down a card, and telling me to spend a ridiculous figure, or he'd spend it for me. I still can't believe he did it— or that I ultimately let him.

I study him now, removing things from a sleek leather briefcase, dressed casually in dark jeans and a snug blue pullover that makes his eyes inhumanly aqua. He begins to pull his sketchpad out of a slim case, and in a gesture I'm starting to find familiar, he runs his fingers over his goatee. My gaze falls on his watch, which I haven't seen until today. It has a thick silver band and a logo that probably means it cost as much as some people's houses.

He glances up to catch me watching him, and leans in to give me a quick, hot brush of his lips. He then offers me my computer from inside his bag.

"Thank you," I say, accepting it, wishing I didn't have to think about the reason I have it.

"What exactly are you working on?"

"Property listings. Boring stuff."

"And what did you do in New York?"

"Research and admin work. Boring."

"What kind of research?"

I hate this. I hate it so much. I just want to tell him everything. "It depended on what my boss had going on. Nothing as exciting as pyramids."

"You like history."

"History that's a mystery."

"Like the pyramids."

This is a connection to my past. I should change the subject. "Yes. Like the pyramids."

"Why a researcher, and not an archeologist?"

"I did what felt right at the time."

"After you lost your family."

"Yes. I went on to college, but . . . I just went through the motions. By the time I woke up, it felt like I just needed my degree and a higher income." I shake off what could turn into a flashback and more information than I should tell him. "Tell me about your plans for the building. What are you drafting today?"

"I'm going to do the underground tunnels from the pyramid to the other buildings."

"Like the real pyramids had."

"Exactly. And glass blocks will create the actual pyra-

mid." He flips his design around for me to see. "I was thinking about A-hole's argument that pyramids have been done,
and he's right. But I have this idea to design two pyramids
on top of the main structure. *That's* never been done."

"I can't picture it."

He quickly sketches a small drawing that's simple, but
enough for me to understand what he means.

"Like you're stacking the pyramids. Can that actually
work? It seems unstable."

"They won't be stacked. They'll be structures within
structures."

"I'm intrigued. I can't wait to see it. I hope you build it."

"If that doesn't win over A-hole, then I'll take it somewhere else and build it. Then you can see it. And maybe we
can go see the real pyramids together."

He says it like I'm going to be around, no matter where
he is, there to travel with him. Maybe I should be worried
that he's become so invested in me in such a short time, but
I'm not. I don't believe the connection between us is something anyone could fake. And maybe I should worry that
he's so interested in something connected to my past, but
again, I'm just not. Right or wrong, I trust Liam, and I'm
hungry for every moment I have with him. I want to find a
way to make it last.

I smile. "So you can seduce me in a pyramid?"

He laughs. "That sounds worth the trip, don't you think?"

My cell phone rings and I stiffen, my playful mood evaporating instantly.

Liam picks my phone up from the table between us and slides it into my hand. "I'm right here, you know," he says, reminding me that he remembers all too well how I'd freaked out over a phone call two nights before.

And it's comforting. I'm not alone. I glance at the number and my shoulders relax. "It's Meg. You met her at the restaurant." Liam visibly relaxes as well, settling back in his chair, and I answer the call. "Hi, Meg."

"Hi, Amy. Did you get the executed lease Luke dropped by?"

My unease is instant. "Yes. I got it. Tell him thank you."

"And you're doing fine? He said Mr. Williams wanted to be sure."

"I am, but I have some questions. Would you have a number for Mr. Williams?"

There's a moment of silence. "No. No number." She lowers her voice. "Luke is weird about Dermit Williams. Apparently the guy is loaded, and Luke doesn't trust me with his info."

"Can you ask Luke to call me?"

"Sure. He's out of town again, though. I swear I'm

going to go nuts in this office alone. How about happy hour?"

I glance at Liam and find his head buried in his drafting pad, his brows furrowed in deep thought, and I want nothing more than to get lost in watching him create his masterpiece. "Not tonight." But I know she holds the key to finding out about my new boss. "Maybe tomorrow, though. I'll call you then, if that works?"

"Sure. Call me."

"And you'll have Luke call me?"

"When he gets back into town."

"Which will be when?"

"Next week."

Next week? "If he calls in, can you ask him for Mr. Williams's number?"

"I'll see what mood he's in."

I sigh. "Okay. Thanks."

I hang up and set my phone down and Liam glances up at me. "Who are Luke and Mr. Williams?"

"And here I thought you were lost in your work."

"I can multitask. I think you know that."

I blush at his reference to the many naughty things he did to me the night before, and this morning. "Luke is Mr. Williams's lawyer, and Mr. Williams is my new boss."

"Who you can't reach?"

"He's out of the country."

He narrows his gaze on me. "Everything okay, Amy?"

I know it's a prod for me to share more, but I care too much for Liam to be any more selfish than I already have. "Yes," I say. If my life wasn't a big circus, and I didn't have this gnawing sensation that I'm about to turn his life into one too, it would be.

He takes my hand and pulls me to him. "Make a doctor's appointment. I want to be as naked inside you as you make me feel. As I want you to trust me enough to be with me."

It is the most erotic, seductive thing anyone has ever said to me. "I do trust you."

And I see in his face that he believes this is a lie, when it's the truth. But it's not about trust. It's about danger.

THE REAL WORLD crashes down on me when I wake up Wednesday morning and the a-hole investor returns and Liam has to go to work. Having showered and dressed before Liam, at his urging and insistence—he would not make his meeting if I was still in bed where he wanted to be with me—I sit at the dining table of the hotel suite, coffee in hand, wishing the clawing sensation in my gut would go away. Having Liam to myself these past few days has been bliss; other than checking my empty e-mail in-box yesterday, I didn't let myself think of anything but him. He didn't give me time. We went to the movies, I had another acupuncture appointment, and we even worked out together.

"I guess it's time to get this over with," Liam says as he walks into the room, stunning in a light gray suit, his shirt starched and white, perfect—like he is to me. My eyes gravitate to his matching gray silk tie and my body tingles.

He closes the distance between us and pulls me to my feet. "You want me to tie you up again."

Embarrassed, I look down. His finger slides under my chin, lifting my gaze to his. "Don't be shy. It's just you and me, baby. Nothing we do goes beyond us. Nothing you tell me goes beyond me."

I wish that were true, but the more I know him, the more I know he'll go after whoever is after me. And they will go after him. "Yesterday you were . . . different when we, ah . . ."

"Yesterday you didn't need me to force you to let go. You were already relaxed. Today, you're on edge. Why?"

I shut my eyes a moment. "I don't know."

"You don't want to be alone."

"I'm good at being alone, Liam."

"I don't want you to be good at being alone. You aren't alone anymore."

"It's too early to make promises like that."

"No, it's not—this thing between us isn't going away. I've had more time in life to figure that out, but you're afraid to count on us. We'll get by those things."

"You're so confident."

"About what I feel for you, yes."

"About everything."

"Not everything," he assures me. "You have this deer-in-the-headlights look sometimes that I'm sure means you're going to run. Run *to* me, Amy—not from me."

I wish I could promise him I will. Instead, I say, "You're going to be late."

He doesn't budge, and the look on his face tells me he notices how I've avoided a promise I might not be able to keep. "Come with me. There's a restaurant and shopping strip nearby you can hang out at, or I'll get you an office to work in."

My heart squeezes at his protectiveness. "I have the doctor's appointment you insisted on, and I have work that I've neglected. Stop worrying about me. You're passionate about your new design and this project. Go make it happen. Then you can stay here with me for a while."

"I keep telling you. I'm not going anywhere."

"Yes, you are. To your meeting so I can make my doctor's appointment."

"I'll drive you."

"It's two blocks. I'll walk. Go to your meetings, Liam."

"I'll be back as soon as possible." He runs his hand down the lavender silk blouse that matches my new lavender shorts, and I feel his touch in every part of me. I don't want him to go.

"Seal the deal." I kiss him.

His hand goes to the back of my head and he slants his mouth over mine, deepening the kiss and leaving me breathless. "I plan to, baby," he assures me and sets me free, grabbing his briefcase and heading to the door. And I know he's not talking about the building. He's talking about me and him, and that sets me in action. I need a plan. A way out of this mess once and for all. Waiting for my handler or someone else to make it go away hasn't worked.

Today I have a mission: answers.

SEVENTEEN

I'VE BARELY LEFT THE DOCTOR'S OFFICE when Liam sends me a text.

How did *it* go?

As well as any appointment that requires you stick your feet in stirrups.

And? he replies.

And I got a sample package of pills. It's seven days before I'm protected.

I can have a lot of fantasies in seven days. What are you doing now?

Headed to walk by those properties and then do some research at the library.

What research?

Don't you have a meeting?

Yes, dear, he jokes. I'm actually being called back in now. I'll be tied up for a few hours but call me if you need me. I'll answer.

He'll answer, I type.

I stick my phone back in my purse and head for the bank. My stop is disappointing. There has been no further deposit, and I worry now that I might have missed a message at the apartment. I find the door free of any envelopes. I should go back down and check the mailbox, but I don't think I was given a key to that. I'll have to get one from Meg.

I'm about to head to the elevator when my apartment door opens, and a big, burly man comes out. I scream and turn to flee just as the door behind me opens, and I run straight at Jared, who grabs my arms.

"Whoa. Easy, sweetheart. What's wrong?"

I blink up at Jared and my hands are all over his T-shirt that covers his rock-hard chest when they should not be, but he is the closest thing to safe I have right now. I turn and glare at the big man in front of my door, who wears overalls and sports a beer belly and some tools, and isn't

240

quite as scary as he was a moment ago. "Why are you in my apartment?" I demand.

"Ms. Bensen?" he asks.

"Yes. Who are you?"

He chuckles. "You know, people aren't normally super happy to see me, but I don't usually send them running into another man's arms, either. But maybe that explains why I'm not dating. I'm scarier than I thought." He holds up a key. "I changed the locks like you ordered."

I let out a breath, and silently vow to make Liam pay for not warning me. "Sorry. I didn't know you were coming today." And how did Liam do this without a key?

I forget the question when I become aware of Jared's hand on my hip, his leg aligned with the back of mine. I step out of his reach and accept the key from the locksmith, who goes on to share some mumbo jumbo I don't really hear.

Finally he hands me a ring with duplicate keys on it. "A maintenance guy came by and said they had to have a copy of the key for the management company. I didn't give it to him. Didn't know him from Adam. He wasn't pleased." He hands me papers and I sign.

"Thank you," I say, and I mean it. "I'll get keys to them." Hopefully never. I don't care if I ever go back inside that apartment, but if Liam leaves, I'll have to.

When the locksmith is gone I turn to Jared, who looks way too amused. "Stop laughing at me," I order. "A single woman doesn't take a strange man coming out of her apartment lightly. No one would."

"I'm not complaining. It gave me a chance to get to know you better. Of course, you almost ran me over in the process. Didn't you know he was coming?"

"I did, but it slipped my mind. I've been busy."

"With the big, arrogant guy from the other day. Is he gone now?"

"He's not arrogant. And no, he's not gone."

"But he's not here now."

"No. He's not here now."

He motions to his briefcase. "I'm headed to a place around the corner to have a beer and get some work done. Want to join me?"

"Oh—no. Thanks. I have some work of my own to do. I just came by to grab a file."

He stares at me, his brown eyes probing a bit too deeply, and I think maybe Liam's right—maybe Jared is interested. I am *so* not equipped to handle two men of their caliber in the same day.

"You want me to walk you down?" he asks.

"Down?"

"To the street."

"Oh, sorry. The key guy rattled me. No. Go on without me. Thanks for . . . everything."

His eyes dance with mischief, and a definite glint of warm brown heat. "At your service anytime."

He turns and saunters toward the elevator, that bad-boy sexiness oozing off of him. I'm not sure why I think the "bad boy" label fits him. It's just a feeling, like the familiar one I normally have with him. But I don't today, which bothers me almost as much as when I do. I'm also not sure why I'm still staring after him when he stops at the elevator and turns to catch me watching him. He grins at me and disappears inside the car.

I WALK TO the properties I'm to report on, and they all seem occupied and well maintained. Everything seems as it should be, but my gut says it's not. At the final house on the list I find an elderly lady sitting in a rocking chair on her porch, and I approach her.

"Hi," I say. "I'm the property owner's assistant, and he just wanted me to make sure everything is fine with the property."

"Howard!" the woman calls.

An elderly man appears at the door. "What, Bella?" He smiles at me. "Well hello, young lady."

"Did you hire a management company or something?" Bella asks.

He frowns. "No. Why would I do that? Been owning this place for ten years and done just fine by myself."

My heart sinks. "I'm sorry. I must have the wrong address. I'll correct my records."

It's official: everything is *not* as it should be. I make a beeline to the Realtor's office, or rather, the law office, and even that is weird. My steps quicken, and it hits me that there's a positive note to today: I don't have that "being followed" sensation.

Answers, however, do not seem to be in my immediate future. When I arrive at the Evernight offices, I find a sign that says "Out to Lunch." I glance at the time on my phone. How has it gotten to be three o'clock? And how is three o'clock lunchtime?

I dial Meg and leave a message, and exchange another text with Liam before I decide to head to the library. In the time I worked at the Central branch in New York, I'd never used its resources beyond looking through some books. I'd been paranoid about bringing attention to myself. Yet then I took the job at the museum. I think I'm an extremist. I sure have been with my willingness to let Liam in my life, and no one else.

I'm walking toward a library I spotted a few blocks away when Meg calls back. "Sorry I missed you. Luke being out of town is killing me. I have to keep running out to deal with tenants."

"Are you heading back to the office now?"

"I have another tenant to deal with. You want to do happy hour? There's a restaurant and bar called Earl's right around the corner from your apartment. One of our customers took me there once. Looks like a great happy-hour spot."

I'll do whatever I have to to find the answers I need. "I'll find it. What time?"

"Five thirty?"

"I'll see you then."

I continue on to the library, still remarkably without the sensation of being followed. I'm not sure if that means I'm without prying eyes, or if I'm calmer now and not conjuring demons where they might not be.

Once I'm at the library, I sit down at a long wooden table and consider where to dig into research. As always when I'm thinking about the past, my mind goes to the tattoo on my handler's wrist. If I find a link to him, I find a link to whatever or whomever I'm running from.

I consider what I've already considered in the past. I've always been certain the triangle shape relates to the pyramids, since my father had done much of his work in Egypt, but I have nothing that confirms this.

I shut my eyes and picture Liam's tattoo. The numbers beneath it form a triangle. I don't like where my mind is going, and I pull my computer out of the small leather briefcase Liam bought me while we were shopping, and Google the pi sign. Nowhere is there a similar image with numbers forming an inverted triangle. And the symbol on my handler's arm was a triangle with words inside—words I'd thought were another language, but later decided was a coded message. It isn't like Liam's tattoo at all. Except for the triangle.

I draw in a heavy breath. Liam's interest in pyramids is a coincidence that's hard to ignore. But lots of people are intrigued by the pyramids, and perhaps he's looking for an answer as to how they were created. Perhaps solving the mystery is a personal challenge. It's a logical interest, especially for someone who mastered his craft at such a young age.

I type "mathematical symbols" into my search bar and scan image after image in hopes of spotting the symbol I'm looking for. I find triangles, but nothing that's a real match—just the same results I always end up with. Finally, I force myself to stop putting off what I really came here for. Today I will do what I haven't had the courage to do before.

I walk to one of the computers with a database of archived material and search for old newspaper clippings of the night my life changed forever. But there's not one single reference to a fire in my hometown in the year and month when it occurred. Nothing. That's just . . . odd.

Back at my own computer, I Google my father and start listing every name ever associated with him that I can find. I'm surprised at how few links I find pertaining to him, considering he was responsible for illuminating more than a few important pieces of history. My heart squeezes as I remember being with him when one of his great discoveries was made. I shove aside the bittersweet memory and refocus on my research. What would make someone want to kill him, and everyone he loved? What would make them hunt me down?

Maybe it's not about his archeological finds. He sat on government committees and became involved in international relations, and not long before he died, there was talk of his retirement from fieldwork and a political appointment in Washington.

I shake my head. I don't know where this is taking me. I was young, and uninvolved in that part of his life. I know nothing about it. But since I'm still a target, clearly someone thinks I know something I shouldn't. It's only logical.

I decide to make a list of everyone I or my family ever

knew, here and overseas. Next, I cross-reference it with the Google searches. I stare at the list. It's sixty names long, and I don't even know what I'm looking for. My first instinct is to mark off everyone that has nothing to do with my father, but I change my mind. I've hyperfocused on this being about him and his work.

It's not about the money. It was never about money. My mother's voice flashes through my memory again. My mind was trying to tell me something, but what? Who was she talking to? Who was there that day?

REMARKABLY, I DON'T have a flashback while doing my research, and I wonder if that has something to do with feeling like I'm taking control and finding answers. At five o'clock I force myself to pack up and head to my meeting with Meg. Finding Earl's Kitchen and Bar is easier than I expect, and I arrive at five fifteen. A waitress points me to the left and I enter a bar area with huge booths that sit on platforms above rows of tables, directly opposite the huge wooden bar. I choose the booth at the very back, where I can see Meg when she enters and I have plenty of room to use my computer while I wait.

I've barely settled into my seat when a waitress appears to take my order. I ask for the house red wine, open my computer, and go still. Jared is sitting in the next booth over, facing me, his computer open and a beer by his side.

I swallow the dryness in my throat as he motions to my table, asking to join me. I nod, unsure why this makes me feel guilty. He's a neighbor, not a lover, but I know Liam wouldn't approve—and honestly, if I found him having drinks with some attractive woman, I wouldn't, either.

He slides into the half-round booth and, to my relief, remains directly across from me. "It's about time we get some quality time together," he says as the waitress sets my wine down beside me.

"I wasn't aware we were trying to get quality time together."

"Well, now you are," he says with a smile, and there is this casual, sexy thing about him that screams *completely relaxed and comfortable in his own skin*. I'm sure many women would be comfortable in it, too, but not me. I prefer the dark edginess Liam wears like an old shirt.

"You really are a smartass, aren't you?" I ask, but it's really not a question. He is.

"Most of the time."

"Why?"

"Comes natural, like being arrogant does for your boyfriend."

Boyfriend? Is that what Liam is to me? It seems too small a word for him. "I'd defend him, but I don't think it would do any good."

"Good call." Amusement fills his dark eyes, and he is absolutely Mr. Sexy Bad Boy in this moment. "What are you working on?"

"Just playing around while I wait for a friend to join me." Avoidance. I'm still good at it with everyone but Liam. "What about you?"

"I'm doing high-tech work on contract."

"You don't seem like a computer geek."

"What do I seem like?"

"The long hair and ripped jeans say . . . something more rowdy."

He laughs. "I'm not sure how to take that, but basically I'm a professional hacker. I'm hired to try to hack a site, and if I can, they then pay me to make sure no one else can. I do a lot of work with defense contractors."

Bad-boy hacker. That fits him. "Thus the Boeing shirt?"

"Correct. Normally I'm holed up in a hotel for a month or so on a job, but a friend was laid off and had to relocate for a job, which left him stuck with the apartment. At six grand a month in rent, he was eager to have someone cover the cost."

"Six grand? How big is your place? I only pay two."

He laughs. "You must have a fan somewhere. There isn't an apartment in the building under six grand. We're prime real estate, in the center of a high-profile dining and shopping area."

"Oh. Well, I think my boss owns the building."

"Who's your boss?"

I hesitate, though I'm not sure why. "Dermit Williams."

"Never heard of him. I thought a big holding company owned the building."

"Hello!" Meg appears by the table, looking every bit the blond bombshell in a snug black dress, and I'm rattled to realize I hadn't even noticed her approach. She hugs me and then glances at Jared. "Good grief, woman, you hang out with beautiful people. I'm sitting with him." She scoots Jared over, next to me.

I'm ready to crawl under the table.

"Please," Jared says approvingly. "Come on in." He glances over at me. "Hope you don't mind getting up close and personal."

Somehow I am captured in his warm, brown stare, and I feel the connection in the pit of my stomach, more in the form of guilt than attraction. Not that I am beyond seeing how hot this man is. He is, and if I were any other woman, I suspect I'd be glad to be here, but I'm not. I'm a woman who is crazy about another man, and the fact that Jared makes me think of Liam speaks of just how intensely drawn to Liam I am. My cell phone beeps with a text, and Meg and Jared chat with the waitress while I pull out my phone.

Where are you?

Earl's. I met Meg for a drink.

I wait for a reply but don't get one. Odd. I shut my phone and stick it back in my briefcase, preparing for a fast departure if I get any more uncomfortable.

"I will be soooo happy when Luke gets back," Meg announces, and I grab the opening she gives me.

"Did you ask him for that number I need from him?"

The waitress delivers Meg's wine and she thanks her before saying, "Yes. And sorry. He won't give it out." She turns to Jared. "I haven't been introduced."

"Jared," he says. "And you are?"

"Meg." She offers her hand and he accepts it. She bats her lashes in a flirtatious way that I've spent too much time staying off people's radar to ever even attempt. I can't see Jared's expression, but I can't imagine there's a man on the planet who wouldn't pant over Meg's immense beauty.

Meg asks, "And what do you do for a living, Jared? Where are you from? Are you single?"

I just about choke on a swallow of wine. Jared laughs. "Tech guy. Texas. And yes"—he glances at me—"I'm single."

I officially have cotton in my throat. I grab my wine and take a big swig. Jared laughs, clearly amused at my reaction. Men like him and Liam send my composure into the Dumpster.

"And how do you know Amy?" Meg queries Jared.

"I'm renting the apartment across from her."

I tilt my head and frown, thinking of my extreme rent difference from what Jared's paying. "He's staying in a friend's apartment. That's probably why you don't know him."

"Why would she know me?" Jared asks.

"She works in the management office," I supply.

"New, though." She seems almost uneasy, but then again, being new is never fun. She adds, "I'm just learning the ropes, and who is where and what is what." She sips her wine. "This isn't what I ordered. I'm going to the bar. Be right back."

Great. Alone with Jared again. And why hasn't Liam texted me back?

"Where are you from, Amy?" Jared asks.

I've been craving a chance to talk to him about my

hometown, yet avoided it at the same time. "New York. You're from Texas, you said?"

"Yes. Ever been there?"

"No. Too many pickup trucks and football fans." Lie. That's part of what makes it Texas, and I miss it.

"And beer." He lifts his bottle and takes a drink. "Us Texans like our beer."

Not this one. "You can keep it. I don't like it."

"Ever tried this one?" He shows me the bottle's import label.

"Never."

"Try it." He offers me his bottle. "It's a different taste altogether."

He wants me to drink from his bottle? "No, thank you."

Meg returns. "Ohhh, I'd love to try it."

He hands her the bottle and she takes a sip. "German?"

"Yes. German."

"Try it, Amy," Meg encourages. "German beers are completely different from the American style."

Jared hands me the bottle, a challenge in his eyes. Somehow, I feel as if drinking from his bottle is some sort of ploy to tear down a wall he thinks will let him get closer to me, but I feel like a deer in the headlights with both him and Meg watching me.

I grab the bottle and take a drink, the bitter taste filling my mouth, and I grimace just as awareness prickles down my spine. I glance up to find Liam striding toward us, his jaw set solid, his eyes hard. He's pissed. He saw me drinking from Jared's bottle.

He stops beside me and takes my hand. "Let's go, Amy."

I'm appalled. Did he really just order me to leave? "Liam—"

He lowers his head and presses his mouth to my ear. "Let's go now."

My emotions are a roller coaster of anger, embarrassment, and more anger. I slip my briefcase and purse on over my shoulder and scoot out of my seat, and I don't look directly at Jared or Meg. "I forgot we had a dinner meeting tonight."

"Amy—" Jared starts.

"Don't," Liam says sharply.

I pull away from him and start walking for the door. I don't have to look to know he's behind me. I feel the predator in him. Well, he's going to find out that this deer in the headlights just grew fangs.

EIGHTEEN

I EXIT THE RESTAURANT AND HEAD to the apartment I swore I wouldn't go back to anytime soon. I've spent too much time feeling like I don't own me, and now Liam wants to own me. That is *not* going to happen. I've clearly been insane over him.

I'm crossing the street when Liam shackles my wrist, claiming control and all but dragging me with him, the big bully. "Let go, Liam."

"Not a chance. Not until we're in my room."

"I'm not going to your hotel with you."

He doesn't even look at me. "Like hell you're not."

"I'll make a scene."

He stops at the curb on the other side of the road and turns to me, his eyes hard, his voice crackling with barely contained anger. "No. You won't." It's a command he expects me to follow, solidified by the way he starts walking again, tugging me along with him.

"Liam—"

"Don't talk, Amy. You'll only piss me off more."

He's pissed off? I'm the one who's been embarrassed and treated like crap. I'm angry too, and he won't intimidate me. He won't control me like this. If he wants to go at it with me, I'm in. Bring it on.

We reach the hotel in record time. The doorman says hello to us and Liam doesn't even look at him, and I'm pretty sure we're a walking billboard for a couple about to go to war. Oh, yes. I'm failing miserably at staying off the radar, and I have Liam to thank for that. No, I amend, I have myself to thank for that. I let this happen. I let *him* happen, and I have to do something about it.

We enter the elevator and he slides his key card through the reader and then pulls me hard against him, forcing my hands to his chest, with nowhere else to go. My legs settle against his, and damn it, I'm wet and aching for him, which spikes my anger higher. He's controlling me, and I don't like it. I can feel him willing me to look at him, and I refuse.

As if punishing me for my insubordination, his hand slides down my back and cups my backside, caressing it deeply, and I feel it like a stroke between my thighs. Barely containing a moan, I curl my fingers around his shirt and I want to scream with the injustice of how aroused I am.

The doors to the elevator slide open and my heart jack-hammers. The adrenaline pouring through me is like acid, burning me with anticipation. The swipe of his card in his door lock feels eternal, and then he's dragging me into the suite's hallway and I'm against the wall.

"Stop shoving me around, Liam! Stop trapping me, and—"

His mouth comes down hard on mine, a deep thrust of his tongue claiming me, the taste of his anger like a shot of spicy, bitter whiskey about to pull me into a haze I can't allow myself to enter. I shove at his chest and he pulls his mouth from mine, and I'm both relieved and tormented by the loss of the connection.

"You had no right to do what you did back there," I hiss.

"You made that pretty damn clear tonight."

"I didn't do anything, Liam. *You* did."

"What I did was have a shit day, which you completed with an exclamation mark." He shrugs out of his jacket and tosses it aside, then does the same with his tie.

"I repeat: I didn't do this. You did."

He leans on the wall. "And you know how I wanted to deal with this shit day? I wanted to get lost in you, and us, and what did I find? You with him."

"He was there when I got there."

"And that made you drink out of his bottle." It's not a question; it's an accusation. His hand slides into my hair, and he stares down at me, his hand moving roughly over my shirt. "I have no right, you say. That's what it comes down to, doesn't it? I have no right to want you all to myself. I have no right to expect you to be loyal."

"You—"

He rips my shirt and I gasp as he unsnaps my bra, teasing my nipple, pinching it. He's rough, hard in a way I've never known him to be.

"I liked this shirt—and now it's ruined," I whisper. But I'm not talking about the shirt. I'm talking about us.

"And you like being fucked. So that's what I'm going to do. Maybe you want me to be the guy I was before I met you. Maybe you want me to fuck you and leave you. Or maybe you'd rather he do it."

"No." My voice is barely audible. I feel defeated. He unbuttons my shorts, and I let him. "I don't want Jared."

He shoves my shorts and panties down my hips and his fingers are between my thighs, stroking the sensitive flesh before the clothes ever hit the floor. "Maybe," he adds, acid in his tone, "we should invite Meg and Jared over to join us."

Hurt and anger overcome me. "Is that what you want? Permission to go back to what you were before me? To fuck everyone and anyone?"

"You're nice and wet just talking about it—"

"Stop!" I shove at his chest. "Stop talking like that, and stop touching me."

He surprises me and lets me go, leaving me standing there with my shirt ripped open and my shorts at my feet. He motions to the door. "You want me to stop. You want to go. Then go."

I hug myself. "Who are you? I don't even know you."

"I can only be me, baby—but I'm not sure you can say the same. I'm not sure you know who you are. I sure as hell don't."

The insult hits a little too close to home, and I slump. "If you wanted to hurt me, it worked." I kick off the shorts and throw them at him. "Keep your stupid clothes and your money and your asshole attitude." I cut around him to the dresser, digging for *my* clothes that *I* bought. I've been alone a long time. I can do it again. I will do it again.

Liam's hand comes down on my arm and he turns me. "What are you doing?"

"Putting on *my* clothes, which don't make me feel like some kind of prostitute you own."

"'Prostitute'? How can you even say that? *You* were the one with someone else."

"I wasn't *with* him, Liam. I was with *you*. *Was*—as in past."

He pulls me to him and the heat of his body, the feel of him pressed to me, is heaven and hell at the same time. I want him. I need him. But not like this.

"Is that what you want?" he demands. "Me gone? Me out of your life?"

I know I should say yes. I should walk away and get myself out of the trouble that is waiting to happen. "You're being an ass."

"Do you want me out of your life, Amy?"

"No," I whisper. "I don't want you out of my life. I want you to stop acting like this."

His mouth comes down on mine and it's hot and possessive, and heaven this time. I sink into the kiss, melt into his body, the argument and the rest of the world disappearing. I am connected to this man. I need him like I didn't think I could need anyone or anything.

I grab his shirt and I pay him back for what he did to mine, ripping it open, letting buttons fly. My hands push under the cloth, absorbing warm skin and taut muscle. I wrap myself around him. I cannot get close enough to him.

He lifts me onto the dresser. I don't even remember him shoving his pants down. There's just his mouth on mine, his hands on my breasts, and the hard length of him pressing between my thighs, into the wet, sensitive v of my body.

He is as he has never been with me. I am as I have never been with anyone. Wild, out of control. He's kissing me everywhere, whiskers rasping erotically over my skin, tongue licking and tasting, driving me insane. His hands curve under my backside, arching me against him, and he pumps into me harder and harder until we are so lost in passion we cling to each other, our heads buried in each other's necks, our bodies moving fiercely, urgently.

The edge of release comes over me in an unexpected, intense rush—too fast, yet not fast enough. I gasp with the clenching of my muscles and then I am there, tumbling into the dark place that isn't danger but pleasure, millions of sensations overwhelming me. In some distant part of my mind, I register Liam's groan, the shake of his body, the tension in his muscles. For long seconds, or perhaps minutes, we just hold each other. Time stands still, and then slowly comes back to me. It is then that I become aware of all the dampness between my thighs, and the reality of what's just happened. Panic rises in me; flashes of fire burn in my mind.

"Get off me," I order. "Get off. Let me down from the dresser." My heart is thundering and my hands are shaking.

Liam leans back, looking baffled. "Amy—"

"Let me go, Liam. Let me go now."

There's a stunned look on his face, but he doesn't argue. He pulls out of me and tries to help me off the dresser, but I don't let him. I jump off the edge and run to the bathroom, grabbing a towel and cleaning myself up. I can feel him behind me, watching me. I can't even clean up without him hovering over me, and yet another eruption of emotion is on me before I can stop it.

I whirl on him. "We didn't use a condom!"

He runs a hand through his hair. "The chances that—"

"*Don't* downplay it. Don't tell me the odds of my being pregnant are slim." My voice cracks; I think I might cry. "There *is* a chance. There's a big chance." I look down and I'm still in my stupid sandals, though all my other clothes are gone. I look ridiculous and I don't care. "I can't be pregnant. I *can't* be."

"Is having my baby that horrible?"

I shake my head in disbelief. "My God. You, who have all kinds of women chasing your money, should be freaked out right now."

"I'm not."

"You should be, Liam! *Everyone* in my life dies. They *die*!

Our baby—" He steps toward me and I hold up a hand. "Don't even think about it. You acted like a total bastard tonight, and this is what happened. This is where it got us."

"I'll protect you. I won't let anything happen to you."

"Do you think my father wanted to let my mother die?" I'm shouting now. I never shout. "You can't protect me. *No one* can." I've said too much, but I don't care. My chest is heaving, my body trembling.

He stares at me, and the torment in his eyes rips through my emotions and creates more. I'm on overload, tunneling into the abyss, and I don't know what to do. Suddenly, I feel him, rather than my panic. He's hurt. He's really hurt. I don't want to care, but I do. "Liam—"

He turns and disappears. I stare after him and fight through a million emotions. I should be furious, but there was something in him just now, during this whole encounter, that I have never felt from him. Something painful.

I grab the red silk robe he'd given me from the back of the door and tie it around me before seeking Liam out. I find him on the couch, his elbows on his knees, his head in his hands. "Liam?"

He looks up at me and there's more turbulence, more darkness. "You're right. I was an ass. My father called today—and that's not an excuse; it's just a fact. I always say I won't let him mess with my head, but he does."

"Your father? I thought he was gone."

"Like I said, sharks swimming at my feet, baby. He only calls when he wants money or he's in trouble. It started out years ago with him claiming he wanted to make amends, and have his son back in his life, but it was only about money."

Oh, God. The way he values honesty makes sense now. I want to go to him, but I'm afraid he'll stop talking.

"He . . ." He scrubs his jaw and starts again. "He was driving drunk today, and hit a car with a family in it."

I grab my stomach. "Oh, God. No."

He nods. "The mother is in intensive care, and the little girl was in the car while her mother almost bled to death. I'd just found out when I went to Earl's. I felt like being with you would somehow . . ." He hesitates. "Then I saw you with him, and I snapped. I'm sorry."

I go down on my knees in front of him, my hands settling on his knee. "*I'm* sorry. I would never make you feel like you did on purpose."

"You didn't make me feel this. I did. I think maybe I have a little too much of my pop in me for both our good. Every time he does this, I crawl out of my own skin. I have to go to New York. I booked the last flight out tonight."

I don't even hesitate in my response. "I'll go with you." He needs me. I have to be there for him. I won't be anywhere anyone will find me. I'll be with Liam. I'll be safe.

"No. His car accident will hit the papers and if you're with me, you will, too. We both know you can't let that happen."

I'm taken aback. What does he mean? What does he know? "Liam—"

"And we've already established you don't want to be around me when I'm like this. I'm not done being an ass. I've got a lot more of my father to deal with, resulting in a lot more of the me you don't like."

"But—"

"Please just stay here in the hotel, where I know you're safe. There are cameras and security, especially in this suite. I need to know you're safe."

He's already decided; I can hear it in his voice. "Okay. I'll stay, but I really want to go with you."

"Stay, Amy. And think about tonight when I'm gone."

"There's nothing to think about."

"We both know that's not true." He sets me aside and pushes himself to his feet, and I follow him to the bedroom, sitting on the bed while he changes into faded jeans, a light blue pullover, and boots, then fills a suitcase.

"When will you be back?"

"I don't know. I have to take care of these people my father hurt, and get him back into rehab."

Back into rehab. This is clearly an ongoing battle for Liam.

"Where's your phone?" he asks.

"I don't know. I don't even remember dropping my purse or briefcase when we came in the door."

His jaw tenses and he leaves the bedroom, returning with my things. "I want you to put Derek's number in your phone. I know you don't know him, but he's like a brother to me. I trust him, and so can you."

I pull out my phone and Liam takes it, keying in the number before going down on a knee in front of me. His expression softens and his fingers caress down my cheek. "For the record, we'd make beautiful babies together."

My breath lodges in my throat and I lean into him, resting my forehead on his. "I don't want you to go."

"I just hope you want me to come back." He kisses my forehead and then digs out the key to the Bentley, pressing it into my palm. "Use it if you need it. I'm taking a cab." He reaches into his back pocket and pulls a credit card out of his wallet.

I shake my head. "No, Liam."

"I'm not getting on this plane worrying that you might need something. Take it. The pin is 1117. We'll both have peace of mind, knowing you have it if you need it."

Reluctantly, I accept it. "Hurry back."

He pushes to his feet, stares down at me for several

seconds, then grabs his bag and starts walking. Fighting the urge to chase after him, I dig my fingers into the blanket and wait for the sound I dread: the door shutting, with him outside it.

I am alone again.

NINETEEN

I WAKE UP THE NEXT MORNING in an empty bed, my cell phone on the pillow where I wish Liam's head was. He hasn't called. He sent me a text when he landed in New York that was nothing more than *Are you okay?* followed by *Going to the hospital* when I'd confirmed I was fine. I called him several times, but he never answered.

Sitting up, I scan the room that has oddly begun to feel like home, but today it's an empty shell and I have nothing to fill it with. It scares me how wrong I feel without Liam. How quickly I've become used to waking up to him.

My phone beeps with a text, and I quickly click on it.

This is why I didn't want you here.

There's a link and I click on it. The headline reads, "Billionaire's Father Arrested on DUI." The subtitle is the worst part: "Mother of Two Almost Bleeds to Death While Young Daughter Watches." I read the article and my gut knots since it all but declares the accident to be Liam's fault for not controlling his father.

I dial his number. He doesn't answer.

I text him. Please call me.

Walking into courthouse is the reply I receive.

He doesn't want to talk to me. He needed me last night, and he feels like I wasn't there for him. *Maybe I have a little too much of my pop in me for both our good*. My confident, talented man isn't as confident as I thought. Somehow the vulnerability in him makes him more human, more special. But he doesn't think so. He thinks of himself as damaged goods.

My hand settles on my belly, and I hate the certainty that if I'm pregnant, I'll have to leave Liam. He's too high-profile, and my child and I would be in the spotlight, where we'd become bigger targets than I already am.

I see why Alex hated the press. Liam is media fodder, whether he wants to be or not.

I don't want to leave him.

I don't want to run anymore.

That means I can't just sit back and hope I'm not found. I can't go on trying to find answers in a scared and non-committed way.

Having made the decision to act, and quickly, I throw off the blanket, rush through a shower, and then dress in jeans, a tank top, and Keds. I leave the hotel on a mission for answers, making my now-daily stop at the bank, where I find nothing has changed. There is not more money in my account.

That fact reinforces my sense of what I have to do next. If Liam were to suddenly be out of my life, I would have to be able to survive and not end up dead.

I swing by the cell phone store, where I buy several disposable phones. A few blocks later, I stop at Evernight, only to find another "Out to Lunch" sign.

I call Meg and she actually answers. "Please tell me you're okay. I tried to call you this morning. I was worried after that man of yours acted like an oaf."

"I didn't see the call." In fact, I'm quite certain there wasn't one, and her lie bothers me. "I'm fine. Liam had a family emergency and he overreacted to Jared because of it."

"Oh no. I hope everything is okay."

I think better of telling her he's out of town. "It's under control. I've been trying to connect with you on the properties I was given to inspect. I don't think I have the right list.

If I e-mail you the list, can you confirm whether I do or not?"

"Sure. Of course." She gives me her e-mail address. "You want to try happy hour again?"

No. "I'm tied up for the next few days. Maybe midweek. I'll e-mail you the list today."

"Yes. Okay." She sounds awkward, but who wouldn't after what she witnessed last night? "You might want to call Jared. He was worried about you."

"I don't have his number."

"I'll text it to you."

"Thanks." *No thanks* is more like it.

We end the call and she indeed sends me Jared's number by text, which I delete. I have no intention of letting him know my cell number, and hopefully Meg won't give it to him. As it is, the mystery blocked-number call has me uneasy.

I grab a few groceries that will allow me to hole up in the hotel room for a few days, intending to do nothing but research. I set up a workstation on the dining room table and then dial Liam. He doesn't answer. I text him. No reply. I try not to think the worst, like he's shutting me out intentionally, or that I'm here due to some obligation he feels to protect me. It's not hard to believe that could be true, with the news piece blaming him for his father's sins.

Guilt, no matter how unwarranted, is his enemy right now.

Settling into a chair at the dining room table, I prepare a notepad and have my computer on and ready. My first priority is to send Meg the property listings. Then I break out the disposable phones. I begin making calls to museums, media outlets, records departments, and old connections linked to my father, pretending to be a reporter from a New York paper doing a story on his life and death.

No one can find any record of the fire. This is illogical. There *was* a fire. I didn't imagine that life-changing event.

Hours pass as I make call after call; it seems like I blink and the room is suddenly dim, the sunlight gone. I flip on lights and check my in-box but find nothing from Meg on the property listings I sent her. I call her and she replies by text. Working late. Will call you tomorrow.

A knock sounds on the door and I stand up, staring toward the entryway. No one knows I'm here. Liam has even stopped the housekeeping visits. I'm not being paranoid; I'm being realistic. This could be a problem.

More knocking sounds, and I decide I'm going to pretend I'm not here.

My cell phone starts ringing, and I glance down to find the caller ID reads "Derek." Good—someone will be on the phone with me if this visitor turns into a problem.

"Hello," I answer.

"Amy, this is Derek. Do you know who I am?"

"Liam's friend."

"Liam's friend who is standing at your door, with a delivery from him."

"Oh. Sorry. I was—"

"Being smart, like any woman alone should be. Let me in, will ya?"

"Yes. On my way." I end the call and go to the door.

Opening it up, I find a tall, good-looking blond man about Liam's age in a well-tailored navy suit, holding plastic grocery bags. He lifts them slightly. "I bring food."

What? "Am I on *Candid Camera*?"

He chuckles. "If you are, we both are, and I think I might be the one getting laughed at." He enters the hallway and keeps walking to the kitchen in the suite. He deposits the bags on the counter. "Liam didn't trust you to spend money on groceries, and he didn't want you to go hungry." He starts putting the food away.

"I can't believe he asked you to do this. I can't believe you really did it."

"He's worried about you."

"He can't keep spending money on me."

He glances over his shoulder. "You do know he's a billionaire, right?"

"Sometimes I wish he wasn't."

He shuts the fridge and leans on the counter, crossing his arms over his chest. "I have to hear this. Do explain."

Liam's words come back to me. *Sharks swimming at my feet.* "How will he ever know I want him, and not his money?"

His expression softens. "He knows, Amy. Believe me, he knows, or you wouldn't be here, and neither would I."

"He won't even take my calls."

"He's messed up right now."

"Over his father."

"Yes. Give him a little time."

I don't like how that sounds. "How long do you think he'll be gone?"

"Just a few days. We have to finalize him as the architect on this project by next week, or he's out. He seems to want in."

"If he gets to use his design."

"You seem to know him pretty well for someone who just came into his life. That's good. He's been alone a long time."

I'm still thinking about that a few minutes later when I shut the door behind Derek, promising to lock up and call him if I need anything. I just hope I don't need to.

I dial Liam. He doesn't answer. No surprise there.

I shower and pull on one of his shirts, and call again. Still he doesn't answer.

TWO DAYS PASS, and Liam has only texted me a few times. I'm going crazy, and it's Sunday, so I'm limited on distractions. I can't make much progress on the phone, and the library is closed. Monday comes with a text from Liam checking on me that leaves me feeling more alone than ever. I dress and arrive at the library when it opens, and my hunt through their microfilm collection takes up most of the day.

Tuesday arrives with another text from Liam that drives me into further research. While I'm no closer to answers about my past, I actually manage to connect with someone who can change my identity completely. The catch: it will cost me ten thousand dollars. The alternative is a flea-market fake that will at least allow me to travel inside the States. At fifty dollars, it wins me over, and I put that on my Wednesday agenda as a safety precaution.

It's nearly nine o'clock when Derek stops by again. I greet him at the door, feeling rather hostile. "Why are you here to check up on me for Liam, yet he can't call me?"

"Amy—"

"Answer the question."

He sighs. "He's dealing with his father's trash talk, and it messes with his head more than you can possibly know."

"Exactly—because he's shut me out."

"He'll come around. Let me take you to dinner."

"No, I'm staying here. Thank you, though." I don't invite him in.

"Liam says you need a job."

"I have one."

He studies me a moment. "Then why does he think you don't?"

"I'll ask him if he calls me."

He sighs heavily. "Call me if you need me."

Guilt over my shortness hits me instantly. "I'm sorry. Thank you. I will."

He leaves, and while I'm no longer hostile, I'm determined. The silence has to end.

I call Liam and he doesn't answer. That's it.

I text him. Call me or I'm getting on a plane and finding you. And if you think I won't do it, you don't know me very well.

My cell rings instantly. I answer to hear, "Amy." His voice is rough, almost brittle.

"I guess your quick call means you really want to stop me from showing up there."

"I don't want you in this part of my life."

He thinks he's bad for me. I think I'm bad for him. "You aren't your father."

"You won't convince him of that." Bitterness and pain fill his voice.

"Let me come there and be with you."

"No. You'll end up in the newspapers."

"And you don't want me there."

"I don't."

I flinch. "Okay. I get it. I'm going to go back to my apartment—"

"No. Shit. Don't. Please. I'm handling this all wrong, just like I did the other night in Earl's. Look, Amy, I'm not the person I want you to know right now. That's why I haven't called—I don't know what will come out of my mouth. But thinking about being back there with you is all that keeps me sane."

My eyes sting. "Just come back," I whisper. "When can you come back?"

"Soon."

"Promise. I know how you feel about promises."

"I promise." He hesitates. "Amy—"

"Yes?" I hold my breath, not sure what to expect.

He lets out a breath. "Tell me you won't leave."

"I won't leave."

"Promise."

I squeeze my eyes shut. If I make this promise, I have to tell him everything when he gets back. He can't protect himself from a danger he doesn't know exists. And I'm pretty certain he'd come after me if I left, anyway.

"I promise."

WEDNESDAY MORNING I'M at the bank when it opens, only to discover my account is as empty as my in-box remains. I'm frustrated with Meg's *out with a client* and *haven't had time to check the listings* text messages. *Surely her boss has to have returned to town,* I think, and I head in that direction. When I find the office closed again, I do *not* feel good about it. I decide to walk to the back door and see if I can get inside to look around.

Once I'm in the small alleyway, I knock on the door, and receive no response. I try the knob, but it's locked. There's a window, and I peek inside to find an empty office, without furniture or even boxes. The window is locked, so I move to the window on the opposite side of the building and find that room is empty, too. Unease goes through me. Something is very wrong about this. There could be another office further in, but from the lobby the place looked very small. I don't know what to do.

As much as I dread it, I know I need to stop by the

apartment and look for any notes. I still have no mail key, since I can't connect with Meg, but I'll check my door.

I arrive to find nothing on my door or under it. Hesitating, I turn to Jared's door and decide to knock. He doesn't answer. Figures.

Deciding to research Meg and Luke, I stop by ink!, a coffee shop near the hotel, to splurge on a mocha to take with me to the room. I've just ordered it when I hear, "Amy."

I turn and find Jared sitting in a corner chair with his computer in his lap, his long, light brown hair loose around his shoulders, and that familiar feeling roars through me more powerfully than ever. He motions for me to join him and I hold up a finger, then grab my coffee and walk over, taking the empty seat next to him.

"I've been worried about you," he says. "After that guy dragged you out of Earl's, I wasn't sure what to think."

"He'd had a family emergency, and was worried about losing it in the bar."

His eyes narrow. "That's your story and you're sticking with it, right?"

"It's my story because it's true."

He closes his laptop and sets it aside, and my gaze catches on his University of Texas class ring. And now I know why Jared seems familiar. I must have seen the ring, and my subconscious registered it. He has a connection to my brother, and an image of Chad flashes in my mind. My fingers dig into my leg. I see his face. I actually see his face.

"You look like you saw a ghost," Jared comments, and I jerk my gaze to his.

"You went to UT?" I ask, and I sound as strange as I feel.

Jared glances at his ring. "I did. Why do you ask?"

"Way back when, I considered attending." Because I wanted to follow in my brother's footsteps, and convince my father I was as good as Chad.

"Why didn't you?"

"New York was home, so it made more sense." It's a lie I tell easily. I'm uneasy about this connection to Jared, but he wouldn't wear the ring if he wanted to hide it.

"How long ago did you graduate?" I ask, trying to find out if he could be linked to my brother.

"I'm twenty-eight, if that's what you want to know."

Chad would be thirty now. "I'm twenty-four."

"So, not long out of school," he observes.

"A few years."

"What did you study?"

"Nothing exciting. Business. How does someone get into hacking?"

"Generally by getting into trouble. I had a knack and did a few high-profile hack jobs just to prove I could. A narrow miss with the law and a close family friend shook me up."

He sips his coffee, and I do the same. "You don't seem to be staying at the apartment."

"I've been in and out at odd hours." I push myself to my feet. "I need to run. Good seeing you."

"Good seeing you, too, Amy. Maybe I'll catch up to you again soon."

I step onto the street, and all I can think is that what looks like a goldfish in the pond could be a shark swimming at my feet. Nothing is right, and everything is wrong. I don't want to pull Liam into the quicksand that is swallowing me, but if I leave, I'm sure he'll look for me, even if it's only out of obligation— and he'll unknowingly put himself at risk.

I don't know what to do. I need a plan, but my mind keeps flashing back to the class ring on Jared's hand. The connection between him and my brother seems too coincidental. They could have been at school together. But what about the empty offices at Evernight?

The pinching sensation in my forehead begins and I swiftly head for the hotel, certain I need to get off the street fast. I manage to get to the hotel elevator before I suddenly see a flash of my brother's face—so clear, so perfect, when I've not been able to picture him for years. That's how powerfully Jared's ring has impacted me.

Leaning against the wall, I will away the image I'd otherwise welcome, praying I make it to the suite without collapsing. My hand shakes as I swipe the key through the lock and then shove open the door. I make a beeline to the safety of the bed and lie down. My cell phone rings, but the spots are before my eyes and I see only darkness.

"Where's your mother?"

Lying on the bed on my stomach, a book in front of me, I jump at the unexpected, unfamiliar harshness of my father's voice, and find him in my doorway. "I don't know. She left a while ago."

"How long ago?"

"A few hours."

"Be more specific, Amy. You know I like details."

The sounds of an engine and tires on gravel signal her return and he is already gone, stomping down the stairs. I rush to the window, parting the curtains to see him yank her out of the car and shove her against the door. I gasp, and press my hand to my mouth. My father has never touched any of us. Their voices lift, loud enough to be heard by the neighbors, but I can't understand the words no matter how hard I try.

I blink against black-and-white dots as a wave of nausea overcomes me and I jump off the bed and rush to the suite's palatial bathroom, going down on my knees in front of the toilet. A pinching sensation pierces my head—and everything goes black again.

I cough against the smoke, flames licking at my doorway, and there's nowhere to go.

"Amy!"

"Mom! I'm in my room!"

"Stay there! We're coming for you!"

I wait, even though the sound of fire eating away at wood has my bones rattling. "Mom?"

Nothing.

"Mom?"

She screams, and I suck in smoke at the horrific, blood-curdling sound, coughing and trying to cry her name.

"Mom!" I finally manage. "Mom!"

She's still screaming. And screaming.

"Mom!"

"Amy!"

My brother's voice rips through the hell I'm living, bringing hope. "Chad! Get Mom! Help Mom!"

"Listen to me, Amy," he shouts, but all I hear is my mother, still screaming.

"Mom! You have to help her. Chad, help her!"

"Listen the fuck up, Amy, I can't get to you! Go to the window!"

"Mom!" I shout.

"Amy, damn it, go to the window or you're going to die!"

My mother is dying. I want to go to her, but the flames

climb closer, inside my room now. On wobbling legs, I go to the window.

"Are you at the window?" Chad shouts.

"Yes."

"Open the window and jump."

I open the window and look down into the darkness below. "It's too high."

"You were a gymnast for years."

"Who quit because I was afraid of heights!"

"Jump, Amy, and make it count. Do it!"

My mother isn't screaming anymore. My mother is—

"No!" I shout. She can't be dead. "I can't jump. I can't jump."

"Jump, Amy. Jump now, or I'll come through the flames and die trying to get to you."

I gasp. "I'll jump. I'll jump." I climb out of the window, look back toward the flames and then forward again. I hold my breath and jump.

TWENTY

"AMY. AMY. WAKE UP. PLEASE, BABY. Wake up."

I blink through a sticky sensation on my face. "Liam?"

"Yes. Thank God. You scared the hell out of me." He grabs a towel and presses it to my head.

I focus on the red stains on his light gray T-shirt. "I'm bleeding?"

"You hit your head and cut it open. We need to get you to the ER."

I grab his arm. "You're here. How are you here?"

"Yeah, baby, I'm here. And I shouldn't have left you alone."

Any reply I might have had is lost to the roll of my stomach. "Oh," I gasp. "I'm going to be sick." I grab for the toilet, and Liam holds my hair back and manages to keep the cloth on my head as I embarrassingly throw up. "I really don't want you to see me like this."

"Nonsense. Can you hold the towel to your head so I can get you some clothes?"

"Yes." I take it from him. "I'm good. You're sure I need stitches?"

"One hundred percent."

I squeeze my eyes shut against the sound of my mother's screams echoing in my mind. And I hear Chad calling my name. *Amy. Amy.* But I wasn't Amy then—I was Lara. Why was he calling me Amy? Is my mind trying to tell me something, or am I so removed from my past that there is nothing but Amy left? *Jump. Jump now.*

"Amy." I jump at Liam's hand stroking down my hair. "Easy. Are you okay?"

I'm not. I want to tell him everything. I want to tell him more than I want my next breath. But the nightmare has reminded me how very real the danger is, and I'm not clear-headed enough to decide what that means for him. For us. "I'm dizzy."

"I'm guessing you have a concussion. Can you stand up so we can get you dressed?"

He helps me to my feet, and I feel pathetic when he has to practically put my shorts on me and then tie his shirt at my waist. He drops sandals at my feet and I slide into them. He puts the toilet seat down. "Sit. Let me call for a car service."

Ten minutes later we exit the hotel, and the doorman pulls open the passenger door of a black sedan for me. My head is spinning and my stomach is queasy as Liam helps me into the car.

"Amy. What the hell?"

Liam and I both turn to find Jared standing there. "Did he touch you?" He glares at Liam. "You son of a bitch, did you hit her?"

"No!" I exclaim. "I fell."

"Back the fuck off," Liam growls. "I would never hurt her, but I will you."

"Amy?" Jared seems sincerely worried. "Did he touch you?"

"*No.* He wasn't even here when it happened. He just arrived and found me passed out."

"Let's go," Liam orders me. "Blood is seeping through the towel. You need those stitches."

I slide into the car and Liam follows, shutting us inside. As he gives the driver directions, I've never wanted to block out the rest of the world as badly as I do right now. He turns

to me and his eyes are shadowed and turbulent. I expect him to ask about Jared, but he doesn't.

"You aren't going to ask about him?"

"You're hurt. It's not time for fifty questions."

"I thought the game was twenty questions."

"I have fifty, but I won't ask tonight."

But he wants to, and now that the miles are no longer between us, I'm not letting Jared get there instead. "I ran into him at the coffee shop today. Other than that, this is the first I've seen of him since that night at Earl's."

"I didn't ask."

"You wanted to."

"Yes. I wanted to."

"I'm glad you're here. You didn't tell me you were coming back."

"I didn't want to promise something I couldn't make happen. I wrapped everything up as I'd hoped early today. The woman my father put in the intensive care unit was moved to a regular room, and I took care of all of her medical expenses and set up a trust fund for her daughter." He grimaces. "My father also moved, from jail to rehab."

"You're a good man, Liam. I don't know why you doubt that."

He leans in and kisses me, his voice softening. "I couldn't sleep last night, thinking I'd get back here and you'd be gone."

"I promised I'd be here."

"And I promised I'd hurry back." He reaches up and holds the towel for me. "We have a lot to talk about."

"Yes," I agree. "Yes, we do." And not for the first time, I wonder if Liam knows more than I think he does.

"Right now, I just want to get you well." He pulls me close and my hand settles on his heart. It thrums beneath my palm, a soothing melody that feels like home. *He* feels like home.

I'm going to tell him everything. I just have to find the right time.

I WAKE ON my side, a bright blast of sunlight illuminating the room, and my eyes lock on to the sight of Liam standing in the bathroom, knotting a red silk tie at his neck. He's been back for two days. One I regretfully slept through, and the other we spent in bed together, but today he goes back to war with his a-hole investor.

We haven't talked much. I was too sick from the concussion, and he was too protective to do anything but worry about me. Despite the ER giving me a thumbs-up on a clear CT scan, Liam is determined to get me to a neurologist. But he'll understand why I won't go when I finally tell him about my past. Or what I know of it.

Liam's gaze suddenly catches on mine in the mirror, and my stomach flutters wildly. He gives me a devastatingly sexy smile, and turns to close the distance between us. I soak in his male grace and the way the gray pinstriped suit accents his long, leanly muscled frame.

"How do you feel?" he asks, sitting on the edge of the bed.

I sit up and touch the small bandage at my hairline, thankfully downsized yesterday from the original gigantic one. "Ready to be out of bed." I stroke my hand down his arm. "Or to stay in it with you." I glance at the clock and note it's nearly one in the afternoon. "But alas, you must go, and I have the acupuncturist showing up in an hour."

"Call me after the appointment and let me know how it went. I hate leaving you."

"I'm fine, and you need to take care of business."

"I'll make it as fast as I can."

A few minutes later he's gone, and I shower and dress before heading to the mini-kitchen to make coffee. The instant I see the dining room table, I go still at the sight of my notepad and computer. I didn't expect Liam to be back so soon, and I hadn't put my things away.

I walk to the table and sink into the chair. My screen-saver is on and my notepad is closed, but I open it to see what would be the first thing Liam would've seen if he'd opened it. I've scribbled *Why is there no record of the fire?* and *Who covered it up?*, both phrases underlined heavily. There are references to my hometown papers, and my father's name is everywhere. I feel sick to my stomach.

Liam might not have looked at these notes, but if he did, he's too smart not to put two and two together. I have to talk to him now. I have to make sure he doesn't do anything to get the wrong people's attention.

I dial his cell, but he doesn't answer. I press my fingers to my forehead in frustration. He never answers his phone.

A text beeps and I quickly glance at it. Just walked into a meeting. Are you okay?

I sigh and type. Yes, I'm fine.

Derek wants us to go to dinner with him and Mike.

Mike is the a-hole. I'm never going to get to talk to Liam at this rate. What time?

Seven. I'll send a car for you.

I'll be ready.

AT SEVEN SHARP I exit the hotel in a white, form-fitting lace dress Liam had picked out during our shopping trip, paired with red high heels and a red purse that I'd chosen. My only other accessory is the white bandage by my hairline that, despite my efforts to sweep my long hair over it and seal it there with hairspray, still shows.

I'm barely in the car when my cell phone rings, and it's Meg. I frown. She's avoided me for almost a week, and she chooses now to call? "Hello."

"I just ran into Jared. He told me you had some sort of a head injury? He said he'd stopped by the hotel several times and left you messages you won't reply to."

Jared stopped by the hotel? "I've been in bed. I had a concussion."

"Was it—"

My defenses prickle. "No, it was not Liam. Jared knows that. Is Luke back in town?"

"Oh, yes. I e-mailed you a new property list. Did you see it?"

"No, I didn't."

"Luke inadvertently sent you the wrong one, and he apologizes. He let your boss know. I guess you were supposed to do some reports you haven't done? Dermit was asking why, so you better get on it."

I'm completely confused. Do I really work for anyone? Is Dermit real or not? "Can you please get me a number for my boss?"

"You'll have to talk to Luke about that."

"Can I make an appointment?"

"I'll get with him and call you."

My phone beeps. "I need to take that. I'll check in to-morrow." I click over to Liam.

"Where are you?" he asks.

"Almost there, I think. I'm in the car."

"I'll be at the door waiting for you."

"Okay. Yes." We end the call, and I immediately pull up my e-mail. The only one is from Meg, with the property list-ing. I have no idea about what is a cover story and what is a problem anymore. The idea of telling Liam everything, and no longer being on my own with this, sounds better every second.

"Your destination, ma'am," the driver says.

The door opens almost immediately, and Liam leans in and tosses a large bill at the driver. "Keep the change."

He offers me his hand, giving me a hot head-to-toe in-spection before leaning close to my ear. "You look good enough to eat. I think I will."

"Liam," I gasp, instantly warm all over, my nipples tight-ening. That's how easily this man gets to me.

Deep, sexy laughter rumbles in his chest and he shuts the car door. "Come with me." He takes my hand and pulls me toward the building, and the way he said "come with me" has me quaking with the certainty that he's up to something naughty.

We enter the high-rise building and my heels click on the fine white ceramic tile. I glance upward at spiraling rows of offices that remind me of a corkscrew, seeming to climb forever. "Wait," I say, and tug on Liam's hand.

He stops and turns to me, following my gaze upward, and then looks back down at me. "You like it?"

"This is the building you designed, isn't it?"

"Yes, this is it. You like it?"

"It's . . ." I struggle for a word that suits it, and settle on "Sexy. Like you."

He pulls me against him. "Sexy, huh?"

"Yes. Very." My fingers curl on his cheek. "And brilliant, also like you."

His eyes darken and heat. "Come with me," he orders again.

We step onto the elevator, and though I know the building is tall, I gape at the panel that offers buttons for floors 75 through 107. "A hundred and seven? That's an intimidating elevator ride."

Liam punches in a code that will take us to the top floor, then holds me close. "I'll protect you," he vows, and I'm not sure he's talking about the elevator ride. I'm not sure anything is ever what it seems in my world.

"Why a hundred and seven?"

"A hundred and five had been done, and seven is lucky."

"You believe in luck?"

"You don't?"

"Not really."

"We ended up seated together on a plane. I'd say that's pretty lucky."

I soften inside, and the warmth he stirs in me pools low in my belly, and slides hotly between my thighs. "I think my luck is changing." The car jumps a little, and I jump with it. "Or not. What was that?"

"The car stops at floor one hundred and shifts slightly to the right. It's part of the sway built into the top of the tower for stability." The elevator stops again. "And just that quick, we're here."

The doors slide open, and I'm glad to get the heck off the car after that jump, planned or not.

We exit into a hallway and Liam indicates another elevator. "The last two floors require another ride up, but I want to show you something first."

"Aren't we going to be late to dinner?"

"No. I told you seven o'clock, and them seven thirty."

We travel a narrow hallway with glass windows from floor to ceiling, and I feel a bit dizzy and unsteady. Liam opens a huge wooden door and motions me inside. I step into an oval-shaped room that is nothing but windows and pairs of leather chairs split by small tables.

Liam takes my hand again. I always have this sense that he's worried I'm about to run away. It's time he knows I'm running to him.

He leads me to the far side of the room, and it's like I'm standing on a cloud, staring down at the buildings twinkling like stars. "It's beautiful."

"So are you," he murmurs, his body framing mine from behind.

"You know," I say, turning in his arms, "Mike might have some merit with the whole 'tallest building' idea. He knows you won't make it just another tall building."

"He knows he wants the tallest building. Period. The end."

He leads me to a chair and seats me, going down on a knee and sliding my skirt up my thighs. I look over my shoulder. "No one is going to catch us," he assures me. "I locked the door."

He cups my sex and suddenly jerks on my panties, ripping them away. I gasp. "Liam!"

He laughs and shoves them in his pants pocket. "Now I have something to think about while Mike runs his mouth." His hands stroke back up my thighs. "It's been too long since I've been inside you."

I blush at his boldness, but I agree. "Yes."

"Did you take a pregnancy test?"

I'm taken aback by the unexpected question. "I told them I might be pregnant at the hospital."

His lips curve. "I did, too. Did they test you?"

"Yes. But they said it was too soon to be guaranteed accurate."

"When can you tell?"

"I think another week."

"Call the doctor and ask."

I nod. "I will."

"Tomorrow."

"Yes. Tomorrow."

"I'm going to give us both something else to think about over dinner." He slips two fingers into the *v* of my body.

"Liam," I gasp. "Not here."

"Yes. Here." And before I can object again, his head is between my thighs and his tongue laps at my clit. Then his fingers slide inside me, and he is licking me in the way that drives me insane.

I grab the arms of the chair and Liam pushes the skirt of my dress higher, lifting one of my legs to his shoulder. For a moment, I drink in the image of me sitting in the chair with this gorgeous man between my legs and me spread wide for him, and it's erotic and exciting, like everything with Liam.

Pleasure builds in some deep spot in my sex, and I swear I just keep on being the easiest orgasm this man has ever given anyone. He touches me and I shudder. He licks and I moan. And that's just what happens. He licks me again, I moan, and then my sex clenches around his fingers. I shatter like glass, in tiny little pieces, pleasure splintering through me until I'm limp in the chair.

When I see my leg over his shoulder, I blush furiously and try to pull it down, and he leans in and licks me one last time. I shudder with the impact and he chuckles, then settles my leg on the floor. I quickly try to shimmy my skirt down my legs, but can't get it.

Liam pushes to his feet and pulls me with him, caressing my dress back into place.

"I can't believe we just did that here."

He leans in and kisses me, pressing his tongue into my mouth before he whispers, "And now we can both have a taste of what the rest of the night will hold, Mike be damned."

TWENTY-ONE

THE CIRCULAR RESTAURANT ROTATES, AND HAS a bar in the center with spectacular views of the city. Liam and I join what will be our group of six, and Mike, Mr. A-Hole himself, greets me with a handshake. Mike is as Liam has described him: rather short—no taller than my five feet, four inches— forty-something, and otherwise quite decent-looking. I say a quick hello to the others attending the dinner, and we're all seated, Mike to my left, Liam to my right, Derek opposite Mike, and two other investors on the other side of the table with Derek.

The first order of business is wine, which I refuse for fear I might be pregnant. "Diet whatever you have," I say, and Liam squeezes my leg, pulling my gaze to his, and there's awareness and approval there. And desire. Lots of desire. I think the idea of me being pregnant turns him on. I think all men get a macho rise out of the idea of creating a baby on some level, but that doesn't mean they're happy when the big belly and dirty diapers come around.

"So tell me about yourself, Amy," Mike encourages.

"I'm a secretary," I reply, automatically slipping into deflection mode. That's who I am, deflection girl, and I am so ready to change that. "I'd much rather hear about you. Were you an investor in this spectacular building Liam designed?"

Derek laughs. "Glad you're along for dinner, Amy." He nods to Liam. "Good call."

Liam squeezes my leg. "I couldn't agree more."

"She certainly knows how to start things out with a bang," Mike concedes, "but she makes my point. This building is spectacular. Let's do it again, a little bigger."

"But you're creating more than a workspace this time," I say. "You're creating a small city, from what I understand."

"This building is more than a workspace."

"A pyramid—"

"Is Las Vegas fodder for tourists," Mike finishes for me.

"Tell that to the Egyptians who spent years creating just one. Tell that to the many scientists and experts who spend year after year trying to figure out how it was possible for an ancient society to build them. And do you really think Liam would build something that would be Vegas-like, unless he was creating it for Vegas?"

Mike gives me a hard look, glances at Liam, and then back at me. "Okay, Amy," he concedes with a smile, "you have a point. Considering the masterpiece of a building we're sitting inside, I can't say I think Liam would do anything that wasn't spectacular."

I grin my approval and our waitress appears. Once she takes our orders, the conversation shifts to the stock market for what seems like forever. Even if I understood any of it, Liam's hand stroking my leg isn't allowing my brain to work. And no matter how many times I clamp down on his fingers, he sets them in motion again, each time tugging my dress a little higher up my thigh.

Dessert finds Derek and Liam in deep conversation with the opposite side of the table, and Mike and I restart our conversation about buildings. Mike points out the many amazing buildings around the world that are of record-breaking height—or were, when they were first built. I quickly remind him that he's forgetting the many amazing structures that garner attention for uniqueness, rather than height.

I glance at Liam and Derek, confirming that they're still distracted, before I dare to be a tad more liberal with my knowledge of the subject.

After we've talked for a good hour, during which Mike appears genuinely enthralled by the mysteries and the creation of the pyramids, I say, "I wonder if you could incorporate a museum into the project you're building, and get non-profit funding to offset the expense."

As I lean back in my seat I suddenly realize that Derek and Liam are gone; I didn't even know they'd left.

"If you're just a secretary," Mike announces, "you're a wasted commodity."

"Ah, thank you." I stare at the empty seats, feeling a frisson of unease. "Excuse me if you will, Mike. I'm going to run to the ladies' room." I push myself to my feet and walk away, scanning for Liam and Derek, but don't see them. So I head for the bathroom to call Liam.

I'm about to go inside it when I hear Liam's voice coming from a balcony across from where I'm standing. I move in that direction and stop dead when I hear, "Did you get the data off her computer?"

"All of it," Derek says. "Including the camera."

"So the camera feed is live?"

"Hot as a day in Texas. Are you sure you have her under control?"

"I can handle Amy. You just get me what I need."

The word "Texas" hits me like a hard punch in the gut. I bolt, my heart in my throat, the adrenaline surge making me shake. I arrive at the elevator and punch the button until it opens, and I all but lunge inside the car. I hold my breath, waiting for the doors to close, certain I'll be discovered.

When the car is finally moving I inhale deeply, willing my pulse to slow so I can think.

This doesn't mean Liam is the bad guy. It doesn't. Maybe he dug into my past. Maybe he's trying to help me. But why would he film me? *Why?* I was falling in love with him. I *am* in love with him. The idea that our relationship was just a facade cuts me deeply. I want to believe in him and us, but I don't dare risk trusting him. I have to survive first, and I need a plan.

Think, Amy. Think. You have to get out of here. Leave the state. Leave tonight. The elevator opens on the bottom floor and I know there are cameras everywhere, effortlessly tracking my departure. I run through the empty lobby, past the security guard behind the desk, exiting the building and immediately cutting to my right. I pause briefly to remove my shoes before running several blocks, until I spot a cab and hail it. I climb inside.

"Where to, lady?"

Where to? *Where to?* My cell phone rings and I know that not only can the GPS chip be used to follow me, but Liam has the money to make that happen. With my heart in my throat, I roll down the window and toss the phone out, my thoughts bouncing all over the place with my emotions.

I need a fake ID that I can't get until tomorrow. And I need to be close to Evernight, so I can try to reach my handler one last time.

I lean forward and tell the driver, "There's a hotel called The Inn at Cherry Creek, in Cherry Creek North. Take me there." I hesitate, then add, "But stop by a twenty-four-hour Walmart first." I need supplies, and a cash machine.

Forty-five minutes later, I step into the hotel room I've paid for in cash, Liam's words ringing in my head. *Run to me, Amy, not from me.* Angrily, I swipe at the tears that slip down my cheeks. I'm not going to cry over him. I'm not going to cry at all.

I dump the contents of my shopping bag out on the hotel bed. A cheap pair of tennis shoes, a couple of tank tops and pairs of shorts, a few toiletries. I remove the wad of cash from my purse that I pulled from Liam's credit card and toss it down as well. Tomorrow I'll clean out my New York accounts, get a fake ID so Amy Bensen won't be traced as having left town, and then I'm gone.

"I'm not running at all, Liam," I whisper. I'm going back to Texas.

Keep reading for a sneak peek of the
next installment in *New York Times*
bestselling author Lisa Renee Jones's
The Secret Life of Amy Bensen series

Infinite Possibilities

Coming Summer 2015 from Gallery Books!

One

RAW AND HONEST.

That's what Liam Stone claimed he wanted from me—but it's not what he gave me. He lied to me. He hurt me. And still, some crazy, stupid part of me clings to the idea that there could be a logical explanation for what I overheard between him and Derek last night. That same part of me that saw him as my hero, willing to fight my proverbial Godzilla.

But he was never truly my hero. And after a sleepless night in the Cherry Creek Inn, I've faced reality. I can't risk trusting him—or anyone else—until I confront the past someone wants me to forget. That means leaving Colorado and my Amy Bensen identity, and heading to Texas, which is exactly what I'm working on now.

Entering the downtown Denver pawn shop on a gust of wind, I swipe my long blond hair from my face and glance around. The T-shaped glass display shelves are unattended, yet the all-too-familiar sense of being watched makes me want to turn and leave. This is where the guy at the flea market, who'd made a cheap fake ID for me, told me I can obtain a high-quality one that will allow me to disappear. And that's exactly what I need because Liam Stone's money and power will enable him to hunt me down and find me if I don't fully cover my tracks.

"Hello?" I call out, hugging myself against the air-conditioning. I'm chilly in the white shorts and red tank I'd bought at Walmart after my dinner-turned-disaster with Liam last night. I hate that I can't go back to my apartment for my things—though most of them were bought by Liam, anyway. Once I'm able to disappear, I'll pull my money from my old New York account and purchase more basics that really feel like mine.

I move farther inside the store, praying the twenty bucks I gave the cab driver is enough to ensure he waits for me. "Hello?" I call again, but my answer is more silence.

Seconds continue to tick by and I feel increasingly

uneasy. Deciding to check on my cab and regroup, I turn toward the exit.

"Señorita."

I turn to find a burly fifty-something man with a thick beard as gray and wiry as his longish hair. "I was looking for Roberto," I say. Is this scruffy-looking stranger my answer to freedom?

He's in front of me now, the scent of cigarettes wafting off him, his jeans and T-shirt wrinkled and worn. "I am Roberto," he declares. He reaches out and lifts a strand of my hair, and it's all I can do not to shrink away from him as he adds, "My man said you were brunette."

I step back, tugging my cheap, oversized purse in front of me and between us. "Wig," I say. "I brought it with me."

"For a quick change of identity," he comments. "Smart Mammi."

I don't know what *Mammi* means, but after the horrid ID his man at the flea market had made me, I'd decided I needed a better disguise. In a worst-case scenario, I can still pass with my Amy Bensen photos.

"Twenty-five hundred," he says.

I gape. "What? No. I was quoted five hundred."

"You need to disappear badly enough to want two hair colors. That means you need the best identification I can make you. That runs twenty-five hundred."

"I don't have twenty-five hundred. What do I get for five hundred?"

"Nothing. You were quoted wrong."

My gut knots. "I don't have that much."

"Well, then," he says, his lips thinning, "use your flea market ID." He turns away, dismissing me.

"No," I say quickly. The fake ID his guy made this morning won't get me through a grocery line, let alone airport security. "Wait." He faces me again, arching a dark brow in a silent question. "I have seven hundred."

"Twenty-five hundred."

My mind races, calculating how much I'll have left to survive with if I go higher. I settle on a firm "Fifteen hundred. That is all I have."

His gaze rakes up and down my body, then returns to my face, and I feel violated. "Perhaps we can barter," he suggests. "You give me something I want. I give you something you want."

My heart lodges in my throat. I want to survive. I want answers. I want to make Amy Bensen disappear, but not like this. "No, I—"

"Yes," he counters, and his hands come down on my shoulders.

Panic rushes over me and a surge of adrenaline spikes through my blood. I shove his hands away. "No!"

He grabs my wrists. "It will be good for you, I promise."

"Let go!" I hiss. A familiar prickling in my scalp begins, signaling one of the dreaded flashbacks that can debilitate me. "No. *No.*" Pain spikes along my scalp like a blade. "Oh, God. Not now."

"Oh God is right," he promises. "Over and over, you gonna say that."

I see the intent in his eyes. He isn't going to make me an ID. He's going to make me a victim, if I let him. I'm sick and tired of being everyone's victim.

I raise my knee hard, putting every bit of myself behind the blow to his groin. He grunts and doubles over, panting in pain. The prickling in my head is more pronounced and I shove against the door, desperate to escape before I collapse. A quick glance to my right tells me the cab driver has deserted me. I run blindly as fast as I can.

Spots splatter in front of my eyes, and I dart into a diner and head for the sign that reads "Restroom." Once I'm inside the one-stall room, I lock myself in and press my back against the door. Pain pierces my scalp and I ball my fists and slide down the door, just in time. Suddenly, I'm flashing back to the past.

I park my Toyota Camry in front of the house, thinking about what it'll be like to be in college a few months from now, with no curfew. Stepping outside into the hot Texas night, I realize that the porch is dark. How very . . . odd.

I frown and shove the car door closed. My parents' Ford SUV is in the driveway. Since my mom isn't on the porch waiting to tell me I'm ten minutes late, maybe the migraine she was fighting earlier caught up with her. Still, I feel uneasy and pull my keys out to be ready.

Quickly walking toward the house, hoping to avoid a lecture, I tiptoe up the porch stairs. The third plank creaks loudly and I freeze. Dang it, this is Dana's fault. I'd told her I had to leave the movie theater thirty minutes ago, but the captain of the football team was talking to her and she's infatuated with him.

I rush up the rest of the stairs, and the instant I hit the porch, a hand wraps around my upper arm. I gasp and a big hand covers my mouth. I reach for it, trying to pry it off of me.

A second later I'm pushed against the wall, the hand still over my mouth. "Were you inviting someone to grab you and hurt you?"

I blink my older brother into view through the inky black night, and his hand falls from my mouth. I grimace and lift my knee to his groin, stopping just shy of contact. "I should hurt you. You scared the crap out of me, Chad! When did you and Dad get back into town?"

He ignores the question. "When you see something unusual

like the porch light being out, don't just charge forward and hope for the best. Walking around in your fairy-tale world of Saturday night dates and teenage gossip isn't going to keep you safe."

My anger is instant. "Teenage gossip? Did you really just say that to me? I want to be at the digs with you and Dad. I want to be exploring the world. It's your influence on Dad that keeps me from traveling with you—so don't even go there, Chad."

A lock of curly blond hair falls over his brow as he shakes his head. "Because I'm fucking trying to make sure you have the normal life I have never had."

His raspy tone of voice sends goose bumps down my spine, and fear clenches my gut. "What's wrong, Chad?"

He just stares at me.

"Chad?" I prod.

He shoves off the wall and scrubs his face. "Nothing's wrong." He motions to the door. "Let's go in."

"Not until you tell me what's going on. And don't tell me it's nothing. Tell me the truth."

"You can't handle the truth. If tonight told me anything, it's that."

"That's unfair. I'm living the only life you let me have. What aren't you telling me?"

A knock on the door jolts me back to the present. I'm on the floor, my legs spread out on the bathroom floor.

"Chad," I whisper, aching from how real he'd felt. Only months after that night, I lost him and everyone I loved. I squeeze my eyes shut, remembering how Mom had opened the door and ended the conversation that Chad never re-opened.

You can't handle the truth. I squeeze my eyes shut, ashamed of how right he'd been. Ashamed at how I've hidden from and blocked everything out for the last six years, afraid of what I'd discover. My lashes lift. Not anymore.

I open the bathroom door and return to the dining area, and it's as if the memory of Chad has shifted something inside me. Deep down, I know this has been coming. Something inside me burns to escape the prison that's been my life. It is almost as if, on a subconscious level, I went to work at the museum to tempt fate and force myself to finally act.

Exiting the diner, I'm remarkably cool-headed about how to deal with my travel limitations. I hail a cab and direct the driver to take me to a bank. There I withdraw the cash from my New York account, knowing I'm sending out an alert about my location to whoever was following me from New York.

Next, I have the driver take me to Walmart, where I buy casual clothes, two small black suitcases, a couple of hats, sunglasses, and basic toiletries. After I pay for the items I go to the bathroom and change into jeans and a navy tee, putting my purchases in one suitcase and leaving the second one empty. Finally, I slip on a red hoodie to make sure I stand out at my next stop.

When the cab pulls up to the airport, my nerves are tight as I force myself to get out of the car. I have a plan, and it's a good one.

I head to the counter of a budget airline and snag a seat on a flight leaving in less than an hour. I check in the empty bag to make my reservation look more legitimate, keeping the other bag with me. Once I have my boarding pass I press forward, reminding myself that there are cameras and security people everywhere. I'm safer here than anywhere else.

Fifteen torturous minutes later I head to the gate, where I claim a seat near the counter so I can call for help if needed. I wait. And wait. And wait. Finally, boarding time arrives. This is where I have to do things just right. I wait in line, and the attendant scans my ticket and waves me down the ramp. I walk toward the entry and disappear onto the boarding ramp, then move to the wall, letting others pass. My hoodie comes off and I stuff it in my bag, then I tug out the black ball cap I just purchased and shove my hair underneath.

An attendant appears from around the bend in the ramp. "Do you need help?" she asks.

"My mother is meeting me, and I'm worried. Do I have time to look for her?"

"You have about three minutes. Is she a confirmed passenger?"

"Yes."

"What's her name? I'll call her on the intercom and check the manifest for her name."

"Kylie Richardson, and thank you."

She nods. "Give me a moment as we continue boarding. What's your name?"

"Lara," I say, speaking my real name for the first time in six years. I don't let myself dwell on the foolishness of using it in an airport where I'm surely being hunted.

"Lara Richardson?"

Brooks. But for reasons beyond my obvious need for discretion, my birth name no longer feels like me. "Yes."

"Okay, Ms. Richardson. Go find your seat and I'll find your mom."

As she goes up the boarding ramp, I follow and peek around the corner to see her walking toward the counter where another woman waits. The waiting area is empty. Like it had been that day I'd met Liam, when I'd thought I was going to be bumped, but instead ended up seated in first class next to him. Now I wonder if that was a coincidence or by his design.

With the attendants facing away from me, I seize the opportunity and quickly leave the gate area. Then I all but run down the cocalator and straight toward the taxi stand. There, I hand the dispatcher a twenty-dollar bill. "I'm late to a wedding rehearsal dinner. I need out of here fast."

He glances at the money and nods. "You got it, sweetheart." He lifts his hand to motion to a cab and then grabs my bag.

"In the backseat, please," I instruct, wanting it where I can get to it if I need to make a fast departure. I can't afford to throw out any more money after the cost of that plane ticket.

I'm just about to get into the backseat when I hear "Amy."

I freeze at the sound of Liam's deep, all-too-familiar voice. No. No. *No*. He cannot be here. He *can't*.

But he is, which can only mean one thing. He's been having me followed—confirming that he was never just a stranger who touched me deeply. He's everything I don't want him to be; everything I had prayed he wasn't.